Glitz

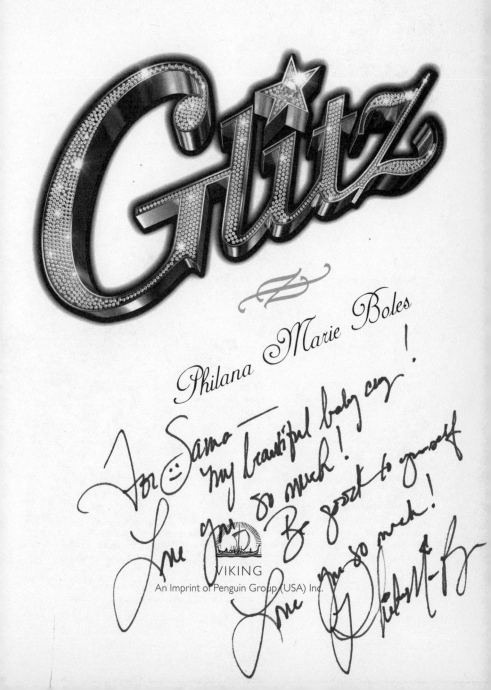

Philana Marie Boles

VIKING

An Imprint of Penguin Group (USA) Inc.

For Sama —
my beautiful baby cuz!
Love you so much!
Be good to yourself
Love you so much!

VIKING
Published by Penguin Group
Penguin Group (USA) Inc., 345 Hudson Street, New York, New York 10014, U.S.A.
Penguin Group (Canada), 90 Eglinton Avenue East, Suite 700, Toronto, Ontario, Canada M4P 2Y3
(a division of Pearson Penguin Canada Inc.)
Penguin Books Ltd, 80 Strand, London WC2R 0RL, England
Penguin Ireland, 25 St Stephen's Green, Dublin 2, Ireland (a division of Penguin Books Ltd)
Penguin Group (Australia), 250 Camberwell Road, Camberwell, Victoria 3124, Australia
(a division of Pearson Australia Group Pty Ltd)
Penguin Books India Pvt Ltd, 11 Community Centre, Panchsheel Park, New Delhi – 110 017, India
Penguin Group (NZ), 67 Apollo Drive, Rosedale, North Shore 0632, New Zealand
(a division of Pearson New Zealand Ltd.)
Penguin Books (South Africa) (Pty) Ltd, 24 Sturdee Avenue, Rosebank, Johannesburg 2196, South Africa

Penguin Books Ltd, Registered Offices: 80 Strand, London WC2R 0RL, England

First published in 2011 by Viking, a member of Penguin Group (USA) Inc.

1 3 5 7 9 10 8 6 4 2

LIBRARY OF CONGRESS CATALOGING-IN-PUBLICATION DATA
Boles, Philana Marie.
Glitz / by Philana Marie Boles.
p. cm.
Summary: Sixteen-year-old orphan Ann Michelle runs away from her grandmother's
house in Toledo, Ohio, with a new friend who is intent on seeking her own fame
while the teenagers follow a hip-hop musician to New York City.
ISBN 978-0-670-01204-6 (hardcover)
[1. Friendship—Fiction. 2. Runaways—Fiction. 3. Grandmothers—Fiction.
4. Orphans—Fiction. 5. Musicians—Fiction. 6. Ohio—Fiction.
7. New York (N.Y.)—Fiction.] I. Title.
PZ7.B635883Gli 2010   [Fic]—dc22   2010024531

Printed in U.S.A.   Set in Rockwell   Book design by Kate Renner

For GXL,
the world's illest MC.
"Rock chinchillas, a'ight?" ☆
Thank you for being my brother.
I love you so much.

⬦ ◼ ⬦

And for Charles Higgins,
king of the 1s and 2s, my
"brother from another set of parents"
who always looked out.
Love you, bruh!

Some people will do anything to get famous. Like Raquel Marissa Diaz. She wanted the world to respect that she was hard like a rock, so she called herself "Raq" for short. It was the first week in October, my junior year of high school when she arrived. I never meant to be her friend. In fact, I lost all my other ones because of her.

By Halloween night, Raq was the only girl I had to hang with. With her daring eyes and those precisely arched eyebrows, it was easy to imagine her as a star. At first I was just a happy passenger on her ride to fame.

Once upon an eternity ago, the place we were headed used to be the VFW 14 Hall, where our grandparents would have BYOB cabarets and boogie to Motown. But this was a new era and that night it had been transformed into the hottest underground hip-hop concert Toledo had ever seen. The Halloween Jam was an ages-eighteen-and-up show and we were only sixteen. But, thanks to Raq, we both got in without being carded. It was like that with her—as if the rules didn't apply or something—and I'd never met someone like that. I'd lived my entire life in a cage and now there was someone holding open the door, saying, "Guess what? You can experience things now. *You're free*."

Standing in the doorway that night, I was frozen, hushed by the thrill of the scene. Hood-rat and swagger-cat packed, the party was just getting started, but already it was deliciously full of the city's most devoted hip-hop heads. Rebels, hustlers, and groupies were everywhere. You couldn't tell who was rocking costumes and who flat-out dressed like that on the regular. It was wild.

Fake cobwebs hung from the ceiling as far back in as we could see. Through all the strobe lights and thick fog from a smoke machine, I could see hints of big, fat jack-o'-lanterns and glow-in-the-dark skeletons. Buffet tables were surrounded with long lines of ninjas, French maids, and pimps. The dance floor was sick! Some folks were poppin' and lockin', while others just stood there confident as they flat-out chilled like they didn't have a care on earth. Shrieks. Howls. Laughter. And an eager ache in my gut. Raq was determined to get us backstage, and I was a wreck imagining what would happen if we saw Piper—a Detroit-based rapper whom I loved more than any other—up close. Would we have a chance to talk to him? And if we did, what would I say?

We were still in the lobby, and already even my skin was vibrating from the bass of the music, a beat so hypnotic that my head had given in to a slow nod. I pretended, as best I could, that I was cool, that this was my club and I owned the night. Yeah. I not only belonged, I was necessary. Me and Raq. World famous and respected. Heads moving and wordless. Vibin'. Coolin' . . .

From what we could hear, the concert hadn't started yet, but the deejay was spinning Millionaire Mal and the crowd was hyped, us included. Never mind that Mal wasn't actually physically there, just playing his music made his presence consume the room.

Millionaire Mal was famous for spittin' stereotypical rhymes, stuff about rising up from the hood and pushing phat whips and owning "thangs," repping the street life to the max. He was dropping lines about hustling drugs to stay sane and I grooved to the bars—one anecdote after another—as if it was real to me, too. Hip-hop was funny like that, how I could listen to the flossiest street tales and relate. As if I, too, knew the pain of having my flesh kissed by a bullet. Please. I'd never even seen a real gun. We were so middle class.

I grew up in a comfortable home with a grandmother who liked for us to sing songs by the piano together at Christmas and even bought us matching holiday sweaters to wear when we did. So, okay, my parents were ripped into heaven before they even got to see me crawl, and I'm sure Gramma was probably just determined to make my life as perfect as possible, but give me a break. Maybe I didn't want that. I grew up never lacking for clothes or money or food or anything. So corny, I know. But I wanted to feel real, like normal people.

And despite my lack of desire to pledge some uppity sorority someday like she had, and also my total lack of interest in even *going* to college and then to get a master's degree in music education like she did, my grandmother was still crazy about me. And I always felt loved. But that's a grandmother's *job*. A girl eventually needs to feel wanted, too. I'd never had a guy to be down for like Millionaire Mal had me nodding my head about. *Yeah.* That was the thing to be. So loyal to a guy that you'll *flap your arms and jump if he says fly, only question asked is how high.*

I wanted a guy like that.

My life was so boring, never anything rough. Mal was going on about the humility of having his electricity turned off, of having to use lighters and matches to find his way to the bathroom at night. For me, there'd always been smoked turkey wings, beans and cornbread, corn-flour tamales, Italian sausage lasagna, or some other hot meal on the stove when I got home, a cozy three-bedroom house for just my music teacher grandmother and me.

Occasionally, Gramma's church-choir friends would stop by

and practice their songs, but that was the most excitement our walls ever saw. I used to have friends over, too, but usually we just watched DVDs or did homework together. Life, for me, was pathetic. Before Raq, I'd never even had a friend who talked about anything in the future besides college. Visions of the future with Raq *never* involved books and academic degrees. We pictured spotlights and exciting cities, signing autographs and arriving first-class at fabulous parties. With her it was okay to love what I loved more than anything. Music. And especially the people who made it.

♯ ✶ ♯

Gramma had her first glance of Raq on the same day that I met her myself. Raq and I were both waiting outside for our rides after school, me for my grandmother and Raq for her foster parents. As soon as I crawled into the passenger side of Gramma's Cadillac, she made a very matter-of-fact announcement. "That child is never allowed into our home," she said. And then she asked if I had any homework. Just like that.

I glanced back over my shoulder as we drove away from school, saw Raq throwing up the peace sign, and I threw one back. Then I turned back around and asked Gramma, "Who, *Raq*? She's cool."

Gramma shot me a look. "Stone. Brick. Or Pebble. *Whatever*

that child's name is, I'd better not find her at my doorstep. Not enough time in the world for me to nail down everything I own." She pulled out of the parking lot. "Child watches the world like she'll steal air from the wind if she can figure out a way."

It was too late, though. Raq and I were already friends.

Earlier that day, because my regular lab partner for anatomy—Corrine Carter—was out with bronchitis, the new girl was assigned to the empty seat beside me. Raquel Diaz— Sister Whitney announced her name—caused an immediate hush as we all looked up at her. She was very pretty, but it was obvious from the way she rolled her eyes that she was also very tough. By the end of that day, every one of us do-good girls rocking Catholic school uniforms was aware of the tattooed rebel (a microphone on her left wrist) new on the scene.

Most girls had to spend four years, or at least three, building up the right to have the kinda stance she took on her first day. With her pink, shimmery glossed lips pursed and her heavily lined eyes, poised to hiss at anyone who dared look at her wrong, the expression on her face said she hated even the way the dry-erase markers smelled in our classroom. She sat down next to me after Sister Whitney pointed her in my direction.

"Hey," I whispered as Sister Whitney began droning on about the day's assignment. Something about coloring in an illustration of the nasty-looking human digestive system and labeling the parts. "Are you new to Toledo? Or did you just transfer to our school?"

She didn't answer. Didn't even look at me. She was too busy studying her acrylic French-manicured nails. Was this girl really going to sit ten inches from me and act like I wasn't talking to her?

I decided to try one more time. "Where are you from?"

"'Nati," she whispered, her voice all raspy and deep. She had chocolate Cocker Spaniel eyes and the longest eyelashes I'd ever seen. With an expensive-looking rhinestone ring, the initial "R," on her pointer finger, she flicked her long dark curls from her shoulder and I got a whiff of a citrus scent, either her body spray or shampoo. She challenged me with her tone: "You been there?"

The attitude and toughness didn't really faze me any. I had a grandmother with a pit-bull growl, and I wasn't about to be intimidated by some new girl thinking she was all that just because she was from Cincinnati, Ohio. Please.

So I just shrugged. "Nope." Then I spilled my box of Crayola pencils out onto our lab table and waved my hand toward them. "Help yourself," I said. Then I began to color.

With a smirk, Raq rolled her eyes and whispered, "You wouldn't last a week where I'm from. Give you one *day* in juvie—let Comic or Spidergirl get a hold of you—and I bet you wouldn't be all nice like that."

As if I cared—I didn't (okay, maybe I did, but that's just because their names sounded cool)—she continued. "Called her Spidergirl 'cause she climbed a wall once to get into a seventh-story apartment. Sliced a girl in her sleep after she crawled in. Comic? Man. She's just funny as hell. Makes us laugh with all her twisted jokes. . . ."

Why would I want to last longer than a day with girls like that? Please. I would never do anything to end up there in the first place.

Raq picked up one of my pencils and filled in the gallbladder quickly before choosing another color for the esophagus.

"Been in and out of juvie since I was thirteen," Raq explained in a quiet tone. I immediately liked that about her, the way she could whisper while appearing to be doing her work. Corrine and I did that, too.

She said, "Got a druggie *madre* and a damn pimp for a so-called daddy. Shoot. Fool foster parents really think they're gonna move me to Toledo and make my life right? These people are straight buggin', actin' like they're the Latin Huxtables or something. Whatever."

Just then, Madeline Berber, a nosy goody-goody girl who was sitting at the table in front of us, must have overheard Raq, because she nudged Georgina Welch, one of my best friends.

By lunch, Georgina was going to make sure Jewel Jones

and everyone else in our crew knew all about Raq. *And* that I had been chatting it up with her. Watch. I braced myself. Jewel Jones wasn't too keen on new girls and especially not *any* girls who rocked tattoos. She got her uppity ways honestly, though. Jewel's family—all jewelers, her grandparents owned Jones Diamonds—are a pretty elite bunch around Toledo.

Raq asked, "So, where you from?"

Sister Whitney passed by our desk then, peering over to check our progress. Eyeing Raq's diagram—a mess of sloppy colors with nothing labeled—Sister cleared her throat but carried on up the aisle.

"Right here in Toledo," I whispered back when it was safe. "Born and raised."

"Whoa." Raq shook her head. "Sorry about your luck. Been in this city a week and already I don't know how you can stand it. What do y'all do to stay awake around here?"

Mostly, I liked music. Really, I loved it. With my friends though, I just spent the weekends store-hopping at outdoor shopping plazas like Levis Commons or Fallen Timbers or going to football or basketball games at St. John's Jesuit— our brother school. No one in my crew cared much about hip-hop besides me. That's just the way it was with them. Sometimes we'd mimic dance routines from videos, and occasionally we'd hang out in Jewel's basement doing each other's facials and manicures or watching DVDs—her house had a real mini-cinema with stadium seats and everything—but that was pretty much it. I realized how whack all those things would probably sound to Raq, though, and so I just shrugged. "Not much," I said.

But glancing over at her wrist—she had a *tattoo*, okay—I got up a little nerve. "Well, I'm kinda into hip-hop."

She gasped. She smiled.

Then she narrowed her eyes a bit and checked me out. "Run-DMC or Beastie Boys?"

Making sure, first, that Sister Whitney was occupied—she was—I replied, "Run-DMC."

"MC Lyte or Lil' Kim?"

"L-Y-T-E." I felt a smile rising across my face. "The scholar MC . . ." Then I added. "But I like Lil' Kim, too."

Impressed, Raq nodded as she picked up a blue pencil and started to color in the liver. "Okay, okay . . . I see you tryna rep some old-school. That's what's up, *chica*. All right, so Fat Joe or Pitbull?"

Madeline and Georgina both side-eyed us. I ignored them. *Who did they think they were, anyhow*? Just because *they* weren't into hip-hop didn't make it a bad thing. "Fat Joe," I replied. "But Pitbull is cool, too."

I couldn't believe it! I could never have had a conversation like this with Jewel or the rest of my friends. Hip-hop just wasn't their thing. The listened to top-40 songs, pop and R&B, but hardly ever rap.

"Good answer," Raq nodded. "You're smart. I like that. I like that a lot. Soo . . . Millionaire Mal or—"

"Millionaire Mal!" No question.

Slap. Slap-slap-slap. Sister Whitney tapped her marker on the dry-erase board, demanding our attention. "I *hope*"— she looked directly at me—"that all the talking indicates your efforts to acclimate our new classmate to the assignment and nothing further."

"Of course, Sister Whitney," I replied with ease.

Once Sister Whitney turned back around and continued writing our homework assignment on the board, Raq quick-rolled her eyes and then smiled at me. As if we hadn't been interrupted, she continued. "Pac or B.I.G.?"

I took a deep breath and whispered back, "Tupac Amaru Shakur."

Simultaneously, we smiled and quiet tapped a high five in the air.

"When I get to heaven someday," Raq said, "I want to marry him."

I gave her a look. "Better hope I don't get to heaven before you, then. If so, he's mine. . . ."

We laughed and then colored in silence for a few moments

more before Raq eventually asked the platinum question. "So, who you reppin' in the underground?"

"Are you serious?" I replied, thinking of all the posters I had of him on the back of my bedroom door. Piper MC was gonna be huge, larger than Millionaire Mal even someday—someday real soon, I had been hoping. "Piper," I said.

He was coming to Toledo in a few weeks for the Halloween Jam. I didn't mention this, though, because at the time it didn't matter. I wasn't old enough to get in anyhow, and I figured Raq wasn't either. That's before I knew that things like age restrictions at concerts didn't mean a thing to Raq.

She grabbed my shoulder and gulped her surprise. Eyeing me with a raised eyebrow, she said, "If it weren't for how skinny you are, I'd think you were my lost sister, for real." She gave my shoulder an extra touch. "When's the last time you had a piece of cornbread, *chica*? A biscuit or something?"

I laughed, lifting the flap on my backpack, offering her a peek at my snacks—red grapes, plums, sour cream and onion Pringles, Hostess cupcakes, bite-size Snickers, and a Twix. "I just don't gain much weight is all," I told her. "Born too early."

"Word? You're a preemie?"

"Yep," I said, thinking about how—after the car accident—I'd been snatched from the womb and spent two months in an incubator while my mother waited for God's hand in a coma. I made it, but she did not. My father had left for heaven instantly when the car they were both in was hit by a tractor-trailer out on Woodville Road.

Raq reached inside my bag and snagged a Snickers, not bothering to ask, which for some reason didn't annoy me even though I usually hate it when people take my food without asking. Maybe because I'm an only child. I never did learn to share. Raq seemed cool, though. Real cool.

She said, "You know what they say about preemies, right?"

I tensed a bit, full knowing what she was probably thinking— developmentally disabled or neurologically challenged. I looked across the room, made sure that Sister Whitney was deep into her conversation with Becky Peterson, and replied, "I'm on the principal's list. Always have been. It's my weight that's the thing, not my brain."

Raq dismissed this with a chuckle. "They say preemies are just babies so ready for life they can't wait to get out." Her big chocolate eyes raced with wonder as she read my face. "That you? Ready for life?"

Already, she had read my mind. *"So ready,"* I said.

"See," she said. "So it's true."

I nodded. "For sure. . . ."

Sister Whitney was making her way back over to our side of the room now and—without saying a word—Raq and I both knew to get focused in a hurry. Sister passed by us without saying a word.

I'd been coloring in silence for a while when Raq picked up a pencil and began coloring the pancreas. *"Gracias,"* she whispered.

I looked up at her, not sure what she was thanking me for.

She shrugged. "You know. For the pencils. . . ."

"Oh," I replied. "Anytime."

So on Halloween night I was sitting with Gramma, sulking like a little spoiled brat. She, however, was content. Any night when I wasn't off somewhere with Raq was—to her—a good night.

At first Gramma had forbidden me to hang with Raq. We had a huge fight about it and later that night I could hear her self-help parenting books on CD playing in the other room. She'd been collecting them since I was born, and I was used to going to bed to the sound of Dr. Sylvia or some other talk-show guru going on and on about how to be a good parent. Or at least how not to be a bad one.

By the next morning, Gramma had proposed a compromise. If I went out with Raq on weekends, I had to be home by midnight. If I went out with her on school nights, I had to be home by nine o'clock. I was to have my phone on me at all times. No drinking. No curse words. And no devil worshipping. Period.

We had a deal.

Now, earlier that night, all I had been thinking was that everyone was gonna be at that Halloween Jam, everyone was gonna get to meet Piper, everyone but me. With Raq at work, who else could I go with? No one. Jewel and them would never go to an underground hip-hop event. Besides, because of Raq, I could no longer even count them as friends.

We had been the Fan (short for "Fantastic") Five.

Me, Yan, Georgina, Deanna, and—of course—Jewel. Thanks to Jewel, ours was one of the hardest cliques to infiltrate. We never even allowed other girls to sit at our table at lunch, even though there were always two empty seats. At football games we *always* had our own bench. Gramma and Mrs. Jones were lifelong sorority sisters ever since their days at Ohio State, and they had traveled a lot together, which is why Jewel let me stay in her little circle in the first place. I had been, I guess, only welcomed by default freshman year. Jewel was nice to me for the most part, but I'm sure if it weren't for our grandmothers being friends, she would have never even said hello to me.

"What's up with *that* girl?" Jewel had said as we lingered in the hallway between third and fourth periods, the day I'd met Raq in anatomy.

"Ew," Deanna had agreed. "She looks like a delinquent."

They'd all snickered about Raq's Louis Vuitton purse. "Bet it's a knockoff."

They rolled their eyes at her expensive-looking shoes. "Bet she probably stole them."

Bet you're all just *jealous*, I wanted to say, but did not.

Our parents—*grandmother* in my case—were all too strapped paying private-school tuition to have us dripped in designer wear, and I doubted if any of us could even walk in those heels, let alone save up enough allowance to buy a pair. Except Jewel, of course.

Noticing Raq's tattoo, Jewel said, "Who actually puts ink in their skin, *permanently*?"

"Biker Girl," they called her, agreeing that surely she was probably only going to last at our school a week before getting expelled.

"Watch your purses, ladies," Yan joked.

"Make that *Klepto* Biker Girl," Georgina added with a laugh.

But it was Jewel who laughed the loudest.

At first, I laughed, too. They were my friends, and maybe they were right. Raq did look pretty rebellious. But then, remembering all the fun we'd had in class earlier, I felt bad.

And then it was Jewel, when she saw Raq sit down across from me in the cafeteria that day, who glared the steamiest from the doorway, instantly launching Project Blackball Ann Michelle Lewis.

What was I supposed to say Raq? "No, you can't sit

here?" There were always empty chairs at our table, so it wasn't like I could pretend there wasn't room for her. And though I'd pretended to agree when they'd ripped Raq's appearance apart in the hallway earlier, really I thought it was unfair. So what if Raq wasn't all conservative-looking like us? She had a way of making me feel like just being me was exciting.

So after she'd spotted me, Raq had taken a seat at the lunch table and pulled a bag of Cheetos from her backpack. From the way Jewel, Yan, Deanna, and Georgina were standing in the doorway, staring in disbelief, it was immediately apparent that I had, by all definitions of the Fantastic Five's unspoken code of ethics, attempted social suicide. Unanimously deciding not to sit with me—or with Raq of course—Jewel had led the others to the other side of the room.

When Raq noticed, she'd said, "What's up with the Prissycat Dolls?"

I shrugged, swallowing a piece of my ham-and-cheese sandwich. "They think they're better, that's all. . . ."

On purpose, I made eye contact with Jewel. *"What?"* I begged with my eyes.

She dismissed me by looking away. Then she pushed away the salad she was eating to further emphasize her disgust.

I sighed and admitted to Raq, "Actually, they're my friends. I don't know. . . . They're just trippin'."

After glancing back over at them, Raq looked back at me. . "*Friends*? Are you serious?"

"Well, our grandmothers were friends," I explained. "And now we are. Toledo's small like that."

Raq laughed an unimpressed laugh. "So let me get this. . . . You're locked in with a bunch of lames the rest of your life just because your granny raced horse and buggies back in the day with theirs?"

"Sometimes they're cool," I pointed out. I thought about all the fun we'd had over the summers. We'd usually spend every single day at Jewel's house and then either head to Maumee Bay State Park or Cedar Point. We all loved the beach and were hoping to save up for Cancun next year for senior spring break.

Jewel's philosophy was: We *are* the company we keep. She didn't like Raq at all and—because I was keeping her company—she was now refusing to talk to me.

Raq looked over at them again, noticed the way Yan was looking her up and down, and turned back to me. She said, "I couldn't possibly care less what those snobs think of *me*." Her attitude was thick. "But if those are your friends, whoa. Some *amigas*, *chica*. Jeez. *Felicidades*."

I took a sip of my apple juice and offered Raq half of an oatmeal raisin cookie Gramma had made the day before. I figured my friends would be over their little tantrum in a day or so, so there was no way was I going to go over there and sweat them. Instead, I made small talk with Raq as she munched on the cookie, nodding her approval. Just another thing we had in common, I realized. We both loved to eat. Jewel and the other girls were always turning their noses up at junk food like it stunk, but I didn't think there was anything wrong with chips and cookies. Neither did Raq.

Part of me sort of wishes I'd just gone over there, tried to find a way to incorporate Raq into our group rather than having to choose between her and them. I mean, yeah, they could be uptight, but they'd been my friends for two years. *She's really cool,* I could have said. *Can you just give her a chance? A week. And if not I won't be friends with her either.* But I didn't.

The next day, none of my old friends would talk to me or even look at me. While we were changing clothes for gym, I asked Yan, who had always been the softest, what it was going to take to end this stupid thing and get back to how cool things used to be. But she wouldn't meet my eyes. She just stared down at her sneakers like tying them was the most important thing in the world.

"Jewel said we shouldn't really, you know, talk to you. Well, until you stop hanging with *her*," Yan said.

"That's crazy," I said, fixing my ponytail in my locker mirror.

"Now I'm not allowed to have other friends? You guys all do. What about Georgina and the volleyball team? And you! You hang out with the art club all the time."

"It's different," Yan said in a dismissive tone.

"How?" I asked, immediately regretting that it came out sounding as if I were begging her.

She didn't answer. And then Mrs. Taylor came into the locker room and blew the whistle so we had to go start class.

At that point, I wasn't willing to back down, and neither were my old friends.

They became the Fan Four, and it was me and Raq against everyone.

Only now it was Halloween night, and Raq had to work.

There I sat in my sweatpants, tank top, and Betty Boop house shoes. Gramma was sitting across from me in her red satin pajamas, one bony leg crossed over the other. Even if I hadn't been a preemie, thin was in my blood. Gramma was just as slender as me. Her perfume, Tabu, was syrupy in the air as she pressed a berry lipstick stain onto her mug, sipped, and then straightened her asymmetrically bobbed wig. To her, this was a fabulous evening.

According to Gramma, Halloween was the devil's holiday, so we played the music loud enough to drown out the *pat-pat-pats* of little trick-or-treaters at the door. All my life, Halloween had always been a bag of candy from Gramma. "Here," she would fuss. "All these kids walking around to strangers' doors, beggin' folks for goodies when I can buy you the stuff myself? I don't think so."

After I'd moaned and groaned for too long about not having anything to do that night, Gramma had set up a card table in the living room and forced me to join her for an evening. We sat across from each other, crunching on Corn Nuts, playing Yahtzee, and listening to Natalie Cole and Whitney Houston songs on shuffle, but I was determined not to smile and so far had not. Gramma noticed this and sang along real loud to the music. She was used to her granddaughter's ways, sulking and wishing for a more amazing life, but nothing was gonna stop her fun.

The taste of hot cinnamon lingered on my tongue, singed from cocoa sipped too soon. Gramma always boiled the cinnamon right in with the milk—the taste was incredible—but I sat with a stone face, refusing to say a word, not even "yum."

And Gramma had been going on and on with her small, annoyingly insignificant stuff. Something about what happened at choir rehearsal. And then something else about an article in Oprah's magazine. And then all about what was on sale at Kroger. Who cared? I was missing *everything.* Didn't she get that? Everyone in the real world was living life to the fullest while I sat at home with my grandmother on a Saturday night.

Gramma had a way of twisting her mouth when she smiled, like she really didn't want to smile but, ah well, if you insisted, and she did that when "Unforgettable," her favorite Natalie Cole cover song, came on. Her round little cheekbones were dipped in rose-colored blush, forcefully shiny. And her tiny eyes glistened against her coal black mascara. Even without company, she always kept her face painted. I should have been polite when she dropped her pencil. Instead, I rolled my eyes and tapped my nubby fingernails on the table, waiting impatiently for her to bend over and get it herself. I hated feeling so mean, but I couldn't stop.

Gramma eyed me. "Enough is enough," she said.

My eyes locked into a stare-down. "You don't under—"

"No!" she said. "Don't you dare tell me what I don't understand."

"I can't go trick-or-treating. I can't go out anywhere like *everyone* else tonight."

"What about Jewel?"

"No." I sighed. "She's too busy being perfect."

Gramma raised an eyebrow.

"Go ahead and say it," I said. "What?"

She sighed. "Mighty strange, you ask me. Two years of high school and now is the first time you have that look on your face if I so much as mention Jewel or—"

"Well it's not my fault. I can't help it if she hates me."

"Hates you, huh?" Gramma appeared unconvinced. "Funny they didn't start *hating* you until Little Miss Gangster showed up—"

"Raq is *not* a gangster. Is that what Jewel's grandmother—"

"Child, I'm sixty-four years old. You think I need somebody to *tell* me what I can see with my own eyes? I don't blame Jewel or your other little friends. I'd run from you, too."

I gasped. I couldn't believe she'd said that. "So you think it's fine for them to judge me, to judge other people? Like they're so perfect. Like *anyone* is so perfect!"

Gramma sighed. "Lord Jesus, help me!"

"Gramma. Really. With Jewel, if she doesn't approve of you, you're not good enough. And if you're not all goody-goody, you're not worth it. But with Raq, it doesn't matter if you're not perfect. It's like, she accepts people for who they are. You feel like it's okay to be who you are and like whatever you like when you're with her. I feel like I'm alive for a change."

"Well, my-my-my . . . All this time it *looked* to me like you were breathing—"

"Gramma! You know what I mean. And she's fun, too. And if she didn't have to work, I'm sure we would be riding past the concert tonight."

"Well, you've got your whole *life* to start doing grown-up

things," she said. "You think this is the last concert Jay-Z is gonna have? Don't you know how—"

"His name is Piper, Gramma. Not Jay-Z."

"Whatever. Do you know how many concerts I went to back in the day? How many times we used to run around chasing behind Smokey Robinson, how many times I sat front row for the Four Tops? Child, please. I know why you *want* to go. But do you think that little rapper boy is somewhere crying 'cause you're not coming tonight? Plenty other fast little hot mamas on the road every night, trust me. Introduce themselves and five minutes later they don't remember meeting 'em." She laughed and began scribbling our names on a fresh score sheet.

I took a deep breath and said through my teeth. "You don't understand, Gramma."

She underlined her name and started writing mine. It looked so simple, so pitiful. Having a fancy name gives a girl the nerve to wanna go big places in life, to chase big dreams in the world, even if she has to journey alone. My life was denied that extra push the minute Gramma requested "Ann" on my birth certificate. Ann Michelle, at that. I grimaced.

My cell phone rang just as Gramma finished writing, and I snatched it from the table. *Please let it be Raq. Please . . .* Her picture ID, a close-up of her in chic sunglasses and a big smile, flashed across the scene.

"Ay, *chica!*" Raq's voice was loud and so was the music in the background. "Just quit my job," she announced. And I could tell she was smiling. Raq had tried and failed to get tonight off, and we'd given up hopes of being able to hang out on Halloween. All of her coworkers either had masquerade parties to attend or kids to take trick-or-treating.

"Really? What happened?" I asked. Raq had only been working at the Five Star for a few weeks. Her foster parents were letting her drive their spare car on the condition that she earned her own gas money. Her foster mother had even hooked her up with a cashier job. Now Raq said she'd had a revelation. She'd be seventeen soon, in five months to be exact, and having a skinny little supervisor—her foster mother's brother, Hal—with peanut butter breath barking orders at her on Halloween was *not* how she pictured her new life.

She said, "Some big ol' musty lady dropped her milk in aisle twelve. So Hal said I had to mop busted plastic and cow discharge or else. *Chica!* Can you believe it?"

Turning away from Gramma, I asked Raq, "*Really?* Like, for real, for real, for real? You really quit?" I had to be careful before getting too excited because Raq had a way of exaggerating, like the time she'd told me she'd hit the lotto when really she just had a scratch-off worth five dollars. I had to be sure she wasn't fantasizing out loud.

"Yup, yup," she said. "No more ringing up peas and babies' ass wipes for me. Never ever. I'm gonna be famous, *chica.* And tonight, we gotta start acting like the very *importante* people that we are. Ay, we *gotta* go meet Piper! You down?"

"G.O.S.," I said as Gramma hummed along to the music.

"Your Gramma is *always* over shoulder." She laughed. "Okay, so don't even mention the party being for eighteen and up if you think she's gonna trip out about it. Just tell her we're going to get pizza."

Raq informed me that she was like twenty minutes away and she was gonna blow the horn when she got here. If I wasn't lame, she said, I'd be down with her. Already, I was sprinting upstairs to my bedroom.

Flipping through hangers, I settled on my new black zip-up hoodie—with the word GLITZ in rhinestones on back—and my pink-and-white Pumas. I grabbed my new damaged jeans and a fresh black tank and laid it all out on my bed. Perfect. If I was going to meet Piper, I didn't want to be in a corny Halloween costume.

Staring at the back of my bedroom door—plastered with pictures—I noticed my absolute favorite photo of my parents. It was taken right after they got engaged. They were at the top of the Empire State Building in New York City, and it must have been windy up there, because my mother was resting her head on my father's chest and, just before the photo was snapped, a bunch of her hair had blown into his eye. He was captured laughing while she was posing and smiling. I always imagined that when they saw the picture with her hair in his face, they'd laughed out loud. And I always wondered what that building looked like. Sure I'd seen pictures of the Empire State Building in movies like *King Kong*, but I wanted to see it in real life, the place where my father had given my mother the ring that she was wearing in the picture. I smiled and pressed a kiss to both of them.

Taped on my door, too, were all of my collected images of the sickest in underground hip-hop. I zeroed in on Piper's face, his chestnut skin, his braids that fell onto his shoulders like happy snakes, and I kissed my thumb and pressed it onto his cheek, just below his tattooed teardrop. Piper was a small-framed guy and still only a rising star, but he was so large in my eyes, and in Raq's. Underground hip-hop heads had already crowned him as heir to the king-of-hip-hop throne and—as history had proven—the commercial world eventually always follows the buzz.

"No need to honk. I'll be waiting by the curb," I said before hanging up, tossing my phone on the bed, and dashing for the shower.

Gramma was shuffling a deck of cards when I made it back downstairs. Solitaire. She saw me standing in the doorway and flipped the cards even louder. She paused to make a face. "That child is going nowhere." She frowned. "Nowhere, *fast!*"

I was so used to this.

She continued to fuss, "And you're gonna be sitting right there next to her too. In a jail cell or on a bench in hell. Keep on."

I cleared my side of the table, wiping crumbs from Corn Nuts into the palm of my hand, and I didn't say a word. What would have been the point? There was no reasoning with Gramma about Raq, *ever.*

Grandma kept scowling. "Can't stand that girl. Little jezebel child. Where do you think you're going with her?"

I emptied the crumbs into the trash. "She's not a jez," I reminded Gramma. "I'll be back. Okay? We're just gonna ride past the concert. Maybe go grab some Gino's Pizza . . . All right?" I had never lied to Gramma before and technically I felt like I hadn't. I mean, we hadn't made it into the concert yet. Maybe we really *would* just drive by.

Gramma shuffled the cards once more. "Listen to me." She narrowed her eyes. "I don't know a thing about how that child was raised but *you*, I do. You just remember that God's only gonna protect you so far. So you go on and be stupid if you want to, ya hear? Test God if you want to. "

She'd say anything to scare me away from Raq. Just anything . . . I sighed. "Okay, Gramma." I zipped my hoodie and snatched up my nylon backpack.

Taking a moment to think, she added, "Now, you listenin' to me, okay?"

"Yes!" I said. "Raq is a jezebel. She's a heathen. She's—"

"Fast as the devil in a skyrocket!" she snapped. "But that's not what I was going to say."

"Oh, sorry! What? She's gonna be an ax murderer or something. Sorry. Forgot about that one."

"I don't know what her profile on *America's Most Wanted* is gonna be exactly, but she's gonna do something. I know it."

"Oh, oh," I said. "Don't forget your favorite. She's gonna get knocked up and have twenty babies—"

"By thirty different men. That's *right*! I said it."

"She's this. She's that. Gramma, *you* don't even know anything about her. . . ."

Her eyes narrowing in, she asked, "Oh? And *you* do?"

"I know she's not a snob. Like Jewel and Yan—"

"That's not what I asked you, child," she said.

I stood silent. "I know enough," I finally said. I waited. "And I know she's really nice to me."

Gramma cleared her throat. "Okay, so let's just say never mind to your grandmother who *doesn't know what she's talking about. . . .* Instead of me saying it, *you* tell me what type of person she is. If you had to ask yourself the questions: *Is this heathen a good person? Is the little dummy smart? Is the little liar honest?* What would your answers be? Because if you can honestly, with all your heart, look your grandmother in the eyes, stand there bold-faced and honestly lie and say—"

I heard the honk and my heart leapt. "Gramma, *please.* . . . Nobody's perfect. Not me. Not you. Not Jewel. Not any of us."

"Who said anything about being perfect, child? I'm just talking about *not being the devil.* You sure don't have to be perfect, but so long as you got an inhale left in that scrawny little body of yours, long as you've got *my* surname attached to yours, you will be decent. You hear me?"

I was so irritated I could have screamed. But doing so would have just made the argument with Gramma escalate and take even longer. And for what? I had never one time in my entire life won an argument with my grandmother. If I had said, "Gramma, the sky is blue and the clouds are white," she would have said, "Child, you don't know anything about life. I've lived a long time and *trust me*, the sky is indigo and those clouds are silver."

Gramma wouldn't even look at me now.

Her hand to her forehead, she only sighed.

I took deep breaths and made a deliberate choice to wait without a word.

In a low voice, she said, "I've lived a long time, learned a lot of lessons. I just don't want to see you—"

"Gramma! You can't choose my friends! You can't keep—"

"Child, ain't nobody trying to pick your sorry little friends! I'm your grandmother and I've got a natural-born God-issued right to call it like it *tiz*! If I wanna—"

"Gramma!" I was fighting tears now, shaking my head and pleading. "Just let up! Will you? *Please*? You said yourself you remember what it was like when your favorite groups came to town," I said. "I just want to at least drive past. Maybe see the marquee . . . Maybe take a picture of his limo or something."

She waited.

I said, "And I'm sorry that Raq isn't the wannabe sorority girl like everyone's precious little Jewel. But Raq is my friend. And some things are more important than all that—"

"Like?"

"Gramma! I just want to go out for a little bit like every other normal teenager in the universe. I just want to have a regular night. I just want to go out with the only friend I have. Can you please—"

Dismissing my pleas with a wave of her hand, Gramma surrendered. "Fine, child. Sounding like I've got you living on a house in a prairie somewhere. Go on. Get on outta here, child, before you ruin my night, too. Go on with your little heathen friend—"

I shrieked. "Thank you. Thank you. Thank—"

"Back in here before midnight," she said. "Or it's *poof*! Just like Cinderella. I'm gonna turn into the little wicked witch on the bike coming to get you. I want you in here by eleven fifty-nine, you hear me? I'll get the mayor to come with me if I have to. You know there's a citywide curfew for y'all little kid rascals anyhow."

Not bothering to remind her that the witch was in *The Wizard of Oz*, not *Cinderella*, I exhaled. "Okay. *Fine*."

"I mean it," she said. "That little clown child can stay out all night and go be a clown in the circus if she wants, but *you*? You'd just better be back here."

On the way out, I accidentally slammed the front door. A thud sounded off as proof that the clock had jumped and wobbled on the wall inside. I waited. It did not fall. Tonight though, I probably wouldn't have cared if it had.

While walking to the curb toward the red two-seater Raq was driving, I fumbled around in my backpack. I was looking— I suddenly realized—for nothing.

My subconscious whispered to me then, *"That was bad. You should have said good-bye. You could have been a little nicer. That's your grandmother. She's all the family you have. . . ."*

Immediately, a voice echoed back at me, my inner Raq: "Chica! *Relax. You'll be back later. You can just be all goofy smiles and corny grins when you get home."*

Raq's horn bellowed as she waited for me to hurry up.

I crawled in, the thump of Piper's bass from the speakers instantly lifting me, the familiar smell of Raq's body spray—a peachy burst of citrus—relaxing me, too.

My friend. My life. And so we rolled.

3

"That store can kiss my plump booty." Raq laughed as she drove. "Both cheeks. Twice." She slapped her hand on her thick thigh as she cracked up some more. She had the kind of body that filled out jeans like a grown woman. Mine, I imagined, would do the same someday. Hopefully. But not yet. Not hardly.

I co-signed, helping her to add insults about her stupid boss. Raq said he could pucker his skinny little lips to her ass. Flipping up the sun visor, she added, "Judge and Kitty, too. My phony *padres* who got me that stupid job and enrolled me in that tormented place."

Raq never referred to them as her *foster* parents, always "phony." To Raq, our school was a horrible place that her new *estupido* phony parents—the "honorable" Judge and Kitty Ramirez—had forced upon her. She said when they'd come to rescue her from the detention center where she'd lived for eight months after beating up her previous foster mother (who, according to Raq, had it coming for taking the money she got from the state to buy stuff for Raq and spending it on herself instead), she took one look at them and had 'em pegged. Anything for image. Anything for reelection. Already, she said, they had an appointment scheduled for a family portrait.

Raq had said she'd roll with all the phoniness at first—she'd use her foster parents to stack up all the clothes Kitty Ramirez was happy to buy for her, drive the car they gave her to use, and also save every dime she made at her part-time job that she didn't have to spend on gas—until she could figure out a plan, but eventually she said she knew she was gonna have to press on from Toledo. She said she had big talent and big dreams and wasn't nothing gonna stop either.

I did the unimaginable, reached up and turned the knob, Piper's hyper and urgent rhymes fading to make the silence too loud. We *never* rolled without the sounds of Piper, but I wanted to hear what Raq had to say.

"Forget them," she said. "Forget that job. Forget this life, *chica*! I'm so tired of cleaning dusty shelves and I am *sick* of sitting around a dining room table discussing life with two of the phoniest people in the universe. They know *nothing* about the real world."

I knew exactly what Raq meant. She was stuck with fake parents and I was stuck with a corny existence. In a way, I could relate to Raq. Growing up sheltered and babied all the time felt just as bad as prison. The only real experiences I'd ever had in life I'd been forced to imagine while listening to music.

"Look, kid," Raq said, her voice thick with authority, commanding my attention. "*Mi nombre es* Raquel Marissa Diaz, yes, but they don't call me Raq for nothing, all right? So let's not ever get shit twisted. I don't answer to nobody! *Nadie.* Not. A. Soul. You hear me? Not for *nada!* Not tonight." She cracked herself up.

I laughed with her. "Got my grandmother on my back. Won't let up. Treats me like a baby. I hear you."

The sound of plastic twisting was followed by a loud crunch as Raq bit into one of those red-and-white spicy peppermints, her favorite. "*Mira!*" she said. "This big old world. You think I can't find somewhere to live? You think I can't pick from all these places to choose from? Shoooot. You got Detroit. You got Sheee-Caaa-Goooo . . . You got places with palm trees and stuff . . ."

"Like Miami," I said, daydreaming, too, of waking up someday and being able to do whatever *I* wanted to do and with whomever I chose.

"Nobody is gonna stop me from making it," Raq said. And I could tell she meant it.

And it was funny. Even when I pictured her on some quiet and relaxed beach somewhere, even with a stupid-looking sombrero on her head, I visualized her hands on her hips and her lips curled up into a frown, her signature *Don't step to me* expression stamped on her face for anyone bold enough to visibly wonder who she was.

"For real," she agreed. "Florida would be hot! But then, maybe I don't wanna have to deal with hurricanes, you know? So, maybe just Los Angeles. Maybe I'll go be on a soap opera or something out there. Sign autographs on cement and press my handprint on the ground like you see on the news. . . ."

I wondered then . . .

What about me? Where would I be?

As if she was reading my mind, Raq said, "And you'll be right there with me. It's you and me against the world, *chica*!"

"Yeah," I said, and I could feel myself smile. "Let's think of other places we can go."

"Anywhere but here, right? Just far away from all the people who look at you when you walk down the street. *Ooh,* there's the girl whose *madre* loved crack more than she did her own little daughter. *Ooh,* there's the girl whose *madre* worked the streets for her own papa. *Mira.* I can go anywhere—just show up somewhere—and what? Raquel Marissa Diaz, better known as *Raq,* is here, I'll say. No more phony judge and his goofy little wife pretending they care."

I nodded along with what she was saying.

"People won't look at you anymore and say *Ooh,* there's the girl whose parents died and left her stuck with an overbearing grandmother. *Ooh,* there's the girl whose friends were phony and too stupid to keep a good friend." She laughed. "Pull the lever on the side, *chica.* Lean back in your seat and take a good look at this boring life we have."

We drove down Dorr Street, and even on a crowded night like Halloween when everyone was supposedly out, the main strip of the city was always free-flowing traffic. Already we'd passed *three* McDonalds and a couple of Rite Aids. Fast-food joints and drug stores. Wow.

She said, "How can I have my life here? Huh? And how can you?"

"Yeah," I agreed, watching the occasional cars pass us by as we cruised.

Then she added, "We'll be grown next year, *chica.* So whatever."

"Exactly." I smiled. "Gramma won't have Ann Michelle Lewis to keep fussing at much longer."

Raq laughed. "Well at least she gets your name correct. Judge and Kitty will be over *Rachel* in no time." Raq said that Judge Ramirez had gotten tired of being corrected and now he just called her "sweetheart." *How was school today, sweetheart? How was work, sweetheart? Do you have any homework, sweetheart?*

"Maybe New York," I suggested then. "They say that's the best place to get famous. I've always wanted to go there."

"Me, too!" she screamed. "It's where it all began. . . ."

That stopped me up for a moment. How'd she know that New York was where my father proposed to my mother? I thought of my favorite picture of them at the top of the Empire State Building. I must have looked confused because Raq nudged me.

"The birthplace of hip-hop," Raq said. "You know . . . the Bronx!"

I felt myself smile. Of course. "I know," I said. "It'd be really cool to see New York. . . ."

"And hip-hop ain't never seen nothing like me," she said. "*Ooh* what I could do to a hook. How much you think chicks that sing hook get paid?"

She wasn't kidding. And boy could she sing.

On Raq's second day at school, she and I had sat together at lunch again—by ourselves—while my old friends pretended not to watch us from across the cafeteria. Raq said she was sick of all the phoniness in the world and that hip-hop was where she needed to be. Politicians, she said, repulsed her and so did all the people at our school. I remember the way my so-called friends had leaned in while they whispered, while they laughed, and how I tried to ignore them while listening to Raq going on and on about getting famous someday.

"So," I had finally asked her, "can you really sing?"

Raq nodded and then washed down the last of her cookie

with a swig of the Dr Pepper she'd scored from the vending machine. She sucked her teeth before answering with a smile. "Wanna hear?"

"Ha!" I laughed. "Of course!"

And then, right there in the cafeteria, in her gruff yet pitch-perfect voice, she sang, sounding as soulful as Mary J Blige herself, "*It's just those rainy days . . .*"

After Raq had finished the entire song, I sat in awe. Finally, I unlocked my jaw and clapped, not in a corny fan-gone-crazy way, but just a few hard ones to let her know what I thought. "Whoa," I said. "That was all that. For real."

Other girls looked over, I noticed, but most just appeared bothered and whispered their annoyance. Jewel, Georgina, Deanna, and Yan were all bent over in laughter, burying their heads in their laps as they cracked up.

"Thanks, *chica*." Raq smiled.

She added, "And you see all these haters?"

I nodded. "For sure."

"That means I did something right. They can't hate if they don't see something they know others will appreciate." She took a long gulp of soda. "Gotta let your haters be your motivators. Jealous chicks always tryna mess with me, but you watch. . . . These here pipes are gonna make me be a star. . . ."

And though she laughed, from the determination in her eyes, I knew Raq was straight-on serious.

"We should hang out," she'd said, jotting down her phone number and email address on a napkin, dotting the "i" in her last name, with a star.

Now here it was, Halloween night, and we were doing more than hanging out. We were going to see Piper! I reached over and turned the music back up. We'd been driving for a while and we were almost at the concert.

Raq had a raggedy spiral notebook full of pictures she'd collected over the years, her makeshift portfolio. She'd showed it to me when I went to her room at Judge and Kitty's one time. They'd done her bedroom all up in pink and ruffles like they'd been expecting a six-year-old. To know Raq was to laugh at that ridiculousness. At the last detention center she'd stayed in, Raq told me she'd had one of the girls in her quad take a few pictures of her onstage during the talent show. In the pictures, she'd worn black leggings and a gray off-the-shoulder sweatshirt, brick-red lipstick, and a white rose tucked behind her ear, a look that crossed between Billie Holliday and that lady from this old movie *Flashdance*. It was my favorite picture of them all and said so much about who Raq was. Stunning and glamorous, even in just a sweatshirt with a flower in her hair.

She said she'd won the contest that night, the prize being a check for fifty dollars. It was the best night of her stay at that particular youth center. And then it was over.

Raq said she'd awoken to the annoying sound of paper

shredding. *Who was up so late? Who was making all that noise?*
Raq told me she had wondered. Then she saw that it was one
of her roommates, the quiet one with strawlike blonde hair,
glaring at her from across the room. And with every tear
of Raq's check, she would laugh. Raq said she didn't even
remember getting up out of bed but that she'd never forget
that girl's screams as Raq whooped her ass. Her other two
roommates joined in and helped beat the girl up, too. Raq,
though, was the only one ordered to what they called "the
pit"—basically a moldy, dark room in the basement reserved
for solitary confinement.

"She was just jealous of me," Raq said. "Like everyone."

Judge and Kitty had a future star in their home and they
didn't have a clue. Raq said she'd never told them about
her singing because she knew they wouldn't care. She said
one day she just wanted them to look up, see a familiar face
singing the national anthem at the Super Bowl, and have to
say, "Hey! Isn't that . . . ?" Raq turned left on Byrne Road and
slowed down as we approached the parking lot. "No matter
what," she said, "we're going to be BFFs—no, *BHF*s, 'H' for
hermanas," she corrected herself, "forever."

"No doubt," I said. "Forever."

"Hey! You're gonna be famous, too," she said. "Those phony
chicks? The Phony Four? Let them see us one day, *chica.* They
go around actin' and frontin' and wishin' they had flava. But

money don't buy you flava. You gotta be born with it. Like us. I clocked them, *chica*. You're better. We both are."

Then she added, "Real true people offer the new girl that everybody else hates a pencil to color with." She winked. "Right?"

I didn't want to be famous, never had. But the stars don't exist without the sky to hold 'em up, you know? And Raq was gonna be a star. Maybe I just wanted to be up there with her.

We pulled up in the parking lot of the VFW and something inside of me knew that somehow, Raq was gonna get us all the way inside. Just then I thought of Gramma. It was as if she was still over my shoulder and I had to resist the urge to look over and make sure she hadn't followed us.

Okay, Gramma, to answer your question, I don't think Raq is a person who does everything right. No, I don't. But yes, I do happen to believe she's going places.

And I know it doesn't seem like it, because all you ever see me do is listen to hip-hop music and run off with Raq, but maybe I'm going places, too. Maybe we both are. . . .

I believe in her.

And more important, she believes in me, too.

We rolled along past all the parked cars in search of a spot, Raq going on out loud about her goals and Piper's music playing in the background. Once we found a place, Raq turned in, shifted into park, and whipped a tube from the silver purse hanging across her chest. She touched up her lip gloss—purple tinted with shimmer—and then flicked her hair. She'd sprayed it with silver glitter, only I hadn't noticed it until then, when it moved.

Raq turned to me and posed, her unspoken request for a quick check. With eyelids glossed in plum shimmer and dazzling metallic hoop earrings, she looked—as she did on most days—like a Latin rock star. Anyone would easily notice her and want to know her name.

"Mega fly," I said. "Better recognize my girl."

"*Muchas gracias.*" Raq thanked me and playfully waved to an imaginary crowd.

Then she tossed the gloss over into my lap. I took the hint and pulled down my mirror.

I studied my lips, plain and dismissible. My eyes, unremarkable. My hair, too fine to give my ponytail much of a punch. All the shiny lip gloss in the world wouldn't get me noticed physically, and there was nothing I could do about it. Still, I put on some gloss, blotted my lips, and swallowed. Raq nodded as Piper's voice danced from the speakers, going on and on about his white-on-white Pumas. Raq turned it up.

On my own, it would have seemed impossible trying to figure out a way to get into that concert. If it were just me alone, I'd have probably just been happy clicking through pictures online the next day and imagining what it would have been like to be there. But with Raq's "Nobody's gonna stop me from doing what I want to do" attitude, I started believing anything really was possible.

She shouted, "Piper's not gonna know what hit him tonight!"

Yeah . . .

I believed that, too.

4

Gramma used to tell me stories about Motown. About Berry Gordy and Smokey Robinson, about the famous songwriting team of Holland-Dozier-Holland. She had a library of books about people in the music industry—*To Be Loved* by Berry Gordy; *Secrets of a Sparrow* by Diana Ross; *Dreamgirl and Supreme Faith: My Life as a Supreme* by Mary Wilson; and countless others—and I'd read every one of them, fascinated with music, the glamour of the industry, the Bob Mackie gowns. . . . Those things I could only read about. But at the Halloween Jam I was actually going to experience something.

Me and Raq stood in the lobby of the VFW 14 Hall as girls—stuffed into excessive hoochie mama gear—paraded by with heads high and shoulders back, trying to walk in heels and looking stupid instead. I rolled my eyes and Raq feigned choking.

She said, "Seeing chicks who try too hard is so disgusting."

I nodded.

And the costumes were laughable.

"If I see one more weaved-out mermaid, I'm gonna need a bucket to throw up," Raq added.

"I know, right," I said. Then I happened to look down, regretting for a moment my stubby fingernails. I tugged at my ponytail. *Oh, well. At least I'm here.*

We glanced up at the bold sign on the wall: COSTUMES REQUIRED.

As if reading my mind, Raq suggested, "You're a B-girl from the Bronx, yo! A graffiti artist." She tapped my backpack. "That's, like, your bag full of spray paint or something."

Latching on to Raq's vivid imagination, I felt a slow rise of a smile. I laughed to myself at the thought of what was really inside my bag. A word search. Some Blow Pops and some Starbursts. Twenty dollars in cash. My camera. My cell—

I screamed. "My phone!"

"What?"

"Raq," I announced as I rummaged through my bag, "I left my phone at home. I think it's still on my bed. I put it down there when I went to change. Gramma started—"

"*Chica!*" She yelled, and with a smile, she said, "Forget about it, all right? You're with me. Who else could you possibly need to call?"

But I remembered Gramma's rule about having my phone with me at all times when I was out with Raq.

"Plus," she added, "if you need to, you can use mine."

"Right," I said. She had a good point. And why would Gramma need to call me anyway? "Okay," I said, deciding to just be over it.

And then, as we waited in line to get into the concert, Raq whipped a tube of glitter from her purse and stretched her arm toward my face. I felt the sticky wetness on my cheek while she worked the tube like a wand, depositing cold and gooey glitter onto my face. When finished, Raq stood behind me and adjusted my shoulders in front of the ticket office. Windows at night turn to mirrors, so my image reflected ТƧITЯA in silver shiny letters on the side of my face. ARTIST, Raq had scrolled.

It was just like her, always knowing just what to do.

"For your costume," she said.

"Sweet." I stared at myself, pleased. "Thank you."

"Of course, *chica*. Anything for my bestie."

Raq, the fearless Latina singing sensation, a costume so fitting.

Me, her forgettable sidekick.

I whispered, "Um, by the way, how are we gonna get in?"

She nudged me. "We will," she said. "Trust."

There were probably still at least twenty people ahead of us in the lobby waiting to get patted down by security. Raq nudged me. "Yo. Look."

My eyes followed her gaze. Offering dap to every person he passed was DJ Hitz from FLAVA 104. He hosted Saturday mornings, "From cartoons till lunch," and had been promoting the Halloween Jam for weeks. To hear him sounding all deep and masculine on the radio and then see him in person was a jolting experience. I had seen him once before when he'd come to career week at school, but I'd been pretty high up in the bleachers in the auditorium that day, so no *way* would he remember me.

Hitz had a voice deep and heavy, but he was straight-up lanky and thin-faced, a real crispy-looking string bean. Tonight, to make it worse, he was clad in a striped prison costume and rockin' a drawn-on six-o'clock shadow. If it weren't for his status, he'd have definitely been categorized lame. But Hitz had ends. Plus, he'd brought Piper to town. He knew what real hip-hop heads wanted to see, and he had helped make tonight possible.

Raq leaned in real close and whispered then, a wicked grin in her voice, "Right there, playa . . . That's money." She slipped her cell phone in my hand and nudged me again. This was her way of telling me not to ask any questions, to just follow her lead. Cool.

Hitz was nodding, smiling, laughing out loud, and chatting as he mingled. He was totally oblivious to Raq's calculated radar. Big—no, enormous—mistake. Poor Hitz.

Once we were up close enough to Hitz, Raq tugged at his arm. His plastic smile still intact, he reacted with a "what up" nod.

Raq feigned excitement and squealed. "Aren't you Hitz?" Her voice was so over-the-top innocent, so giddy and completely unlike her, that it shocked me for a moment. That girl was a natural.

Hitz looked proud. "In the flesh . . ."

"Yo! I *thought* that was you!" Raq jumped up and down a couple of times, then offered an animated head roll, like she could hardly believe her luck. "Ooh whee! You don't understand . . . I'm, like, your biggest fan!"

Hitz reminded me of a skinny chicken when he laughed.

Real quick, Raq offered me a wink. My cue.

"Yes," I said, "my girl *loves* you!"

She asked him, "Mind if she snaps our picture?"

"My pleasure, *mami*," Hitz said, his accent sounding straight-up stupid. He stepped in and put his arm around a grinning Raq. I tried hard not to laugh, but I had to as I whipped out her cell phone and clicked a picture. He probably thought I was just excited, too. Ha!

"I listen to your show, like, all the time!" Raq told Hitz.

"Right on . . ."

"You crack me up!"

"That's what I do, baby."

"104 is my *favorite* station, too."

"Well, you know what it is . . . Keep it locked."

"Oh my goodness. I just can't believe it. It's really you. *Mira* . . . One day I'm gonna be a famous singer. You're gonna be playing my songs."

That's when Hitz's smile faded. This had to be the side of the groupie attention that annoyed him. Loved the ego stroking. Hated the coattail riders. Was Raq fan or fake? For real or just tryin' to get on? Hitz's face changed and his jaw bone clenched as he tried to figure it out. He said, "Oh yeah?"

Knowing she'd tripped a bit, Raq went in for the kill. She eyed the poster on the wall and waited for Hitz's gaze to follow. Red, black, white, and glossy, the design showed a giant fist bursting through a brick wall, the words demanding WHO ROCKS THE MIC? At the bottom was a montage of pictures of talent slated to perform that night. Piper and all his braids were bottom left.

"It's the hottest night in the city," she said. "And *you're* the hottest deejay. You gotta have the 411 on the after party. Yo, don't front. I know y'all are having one."

Hitz took a moment to really study who he was talking to. If she wanted to be down, what was he gonna get in return? He replied, "You 'bout what, sixteen, seventeen?"

"Yeah, *right*!" Raq shook her head and proceeded to lie. "Twenty. Well, next week I'll be. I'm actually nineteen."

He relaxed his face, no more silly chicken, and in all seriousness leaned in to Raq. They whispered back and forth to each other, their voices now muted to my ears. With Raq focused on her mission, I slipped her phone back in my pocket and diverted my attention to watching the crowd.

I noticed a group of girls glaring at Raq. *Who is that*? I imagined them pondering. *And why is she all up on Hitz?* One girl, dressed like Queen Hoochie—I *hope* that was a costume—and her crew of bees stood posted up against the wall, looking annoyed, making comments back and forth, offering occasional dry chuckles as they did. I just shook my head and looked away. None of them would ever be as fly as Raq. Must have sucked for them to stand there recognizing that. I laughed to myself, wishing Georgina and Jewel could see me now, Yan and Deanna, too. I was fine without them. Better than fine.

Raq had completely lured in Hitz, her mouth pressed in close to his cheek as she whispered things that made him laugh a lot and then nod. Must have been working. No way would she have wasted this much time if it weren't.

And just like that, we ditched the line and walked into the party with Hitz. No one, of course, asked for his ID, and so no one therefore asked for ours, either. We didn't even have to get searched like all the others. As a matter of fact, we didn't even have to pay.

Once inside the party, Raq called over to me, "*Chica*, you got my phone?"

Hitz was grinning, no doubt looking forward to whatever Raq had promised him in exchange for getting us into the concert. I gave Raq back her phone and she programmed Hitz's number in.

"All right then, love," I heard him say as he held his hand to his face as if it were a phone. "I got business now. Just hit me up later. Tonight."

Raq's nod was so mellow. "Okay," she said. "That's what's up."

With Hitz gone, Raq linked her eyes with mine. She gestured toward the belly of the party and off we went. We settled on a spot behind a Miss Piggy and a Frankenstein, an area where a bunch of people were passing out free CDs. Raq checked over her shoulder before raising her voice above the music, loud enough for just me to hear.

"Yo, *chica!*" she said. "You know I swallowed that fool whole, kicking and still breathing, right? Tell you like this . . . The world ain't ready for us!" She whipped something from her pocket and pressed weight into the palm of my hand.

I looked down. With hologram effects, three magic letters screamed up at me: VIP. And underneath that was the word PASS. There was also a picture of Piper, iced out in jewels, his wild braids dancing atop his head, landing occasionally onto his shoulders. I couldn't believe it! Raq had clipped Hitz of his backstage credentials. That poor fool was walking around exchanging dap and posing for pictures with nothing but an empty plastic case hanging from string around his neck. He was gonna be livid.

Part of me felt bad. She had actually just *stolen* something. Whoa. Not cool at all.

But then another part of me just brushed it off as I imagined her words.

It's just a backstage pass, chica. *It's not that serious.*

◻ ◼ ◻

"She's with me!" Raq spat a warning to the overweight and overworked-looking security guard manning backstage. He'd waved her through, sure. But Raq had the pass. He'd stopped me with a glare and a *tsk-tsk-tsk* sound as he shook his head.

"One pass. One person," he'd said.

Then Raq negotiated. "How much says she can come, too?"

He looked me over. "Half a bill."

Raq smacked her lips. "Fool, pa-leeze! Lean back."

"Look," he was annoyed. "I'm gonna need y'all to clear this area. You're either backstage or in the house. What's it gonna be?"

Raq rolled her eyes. "Thirty," she countered. "Don't trip."

I could tell he was a bit impressed with Raq, his reluctant

smirk said it all. Still, he shrugged. "Forty-five," he said. "Or keep steppin'."

Raq was holding a knot in her hand and I wondered where she'd gotten so much money from. If she was stacking ends like that at the grocery store, maybe I needed to ask Gramma if I could work part-time, too. Raq counted out forty-five dollars and the security guard snatched the money she presented before waving me in.

"Whack security guard is gonna regret treating us like that when I'm headlining one day," Raq said. "Watch."

Backstage felt like a dimly lit sauna but no one seemed to care. Happy chaos filled the scene. People talking too loud, laughing too hard, just hyped. Raq tapped my shoulder again and again, harder and harder. "This is it," she'd say. Or, "This is what it's like, *chica!*" She led me through the dark maze as if she'd done this before, like she knew where she was going and what to do backstage. I had no clue and just followed her lead.

The last concert I'd gone to was sophomore year when Kelly Clarkson was at the Palace of Auburn Hills in Michigan and Jewel's grandmother drove us the nearly two hours to get there. Hip-hop, though? Live and in person? This was a whole new world for me. Still, I felt immediately at home. This was our night, mine and Raq's. Our life. And we were here to enjoy it!

Raq and I had to shoulder and shove our way through pockets of people, some of whom looked weirdly familiar. *Was that DJ JD from "Hip-Hop After Dark"?* Had to be! I recognized her gap-toothed easy smile from the billboard downtown.

We even got cussed at once for bumping into some dude setting up a camera stand. Finally, we made our way through all the radio personalities, entourages, and random groupies, and settled in the wing of the stage. Looking up those big royal blue curtains, fat heavy ropes hanging, was a delicious reminder that we were officially backstage. Just then a red spotlight blasted the stage and the heat really ignited.

DJ Kindred, the emcee for the evening, appeared, mic in hand, trying in vain to hush the crowd. We were just a few feet away from him, but his words were barely audible. People were out there going bananas. I just barely managed to hear him say that Piper would be next to perform. Raq and I linked arms, laughing, crunk beyond belief. DJ Kindred said there were two more performers that would appear after him—no doubt Woody Wood was going to be the main attraction—but Piper was *our* headliner. And look at us! We'd made it just in time and were in prime position for his show.

Ripples of screams filled the room full of underground hip-hop heads, the most passionate of any type of music fans. We didn't love performers like Piper just because they were on television or in mainstream magazines, we loved their music for real.

A hand touched my waist from behind and the warm smell of liquor was heavy on my neck. The voice said, "Yo, Glitz. Pardon me, ma."

Sure, his braids were pulled back into a chubby ponytail.

And yes, those tiny little eyes were narrow and tense.

But it was him. Definitely.

And he was looking. At me.

The tattooed teardrop . . .

Those flawless white teeth . . .

But who in the world was Glitz?

His hand lingering on my waist, I suddenly remembered my zip-up hoodie, the word *Glitz* in rhinestones on the back. I accepted the shudder in my chest but was annoyed by the heaviness in my feet. Why couldn't I do what he so obviously wanted me to? Why couldn't I just. Move. Over.

Someone else pressed a hand on my shoulder and barked, "Move!" This time I did.

I was unblinking, unbreathing, unthinking and, I'm sure, absolutely uncool.

I said nothing. I could only look at Piper as he walked deeper into the wing toward the stage. I heard Raq say, "Wow. . . ." And then, *"Dayum."*

Dressed in all white, from the bandana around his neck to his impossibly clean work boots, Piper had eased past us, but his presence had been so magnetic that following him almost seemed like something I was *supposed* to do, like I was meant to be around him.

A crew of men, about five or six, were rocking gold hoodies and old-school shell-toed Adidas. They followed behind Piper, all of them offering pissed-off game faces at everyone they passed, including me. Funny. They were all trying to be so hard, look so cool, yet Piper had been breezy like the wind, his smile full wattage like the sun. They all stood at the helm of the stage as Piper awaited his cue, fists frozen in the air as they waited, Piper's loyal militia. And then . . .

5

Nee, nee-ne-nee-nee.

Nee, nee-nee-nee nee . . .

Oh, the sound was so electric! Such a contrast from the hard bass thuds of Millionaire Mal. Piper's beats were always unique, but this song, with an electric guitar as the main instrument, was the most unusual. It sounded more like heavy rock, without even a hint of stereotypical hip-hop bass. No one in hip-hop would *dare* spit over such a sound. Only Piper. The hungriest underdog in the junkyard. Mainstream success had nothing on underground love.

His hype men right behind him, Piper stood waiting like the pro that he was. Calm, despite the crowd losing their minds. Patient. Too impossibly cool. He glanced back at one of his hype men, nodded, and flashed that smile. This was his type of crowd and he was gonna give it to 'em!

Then Piper turned and bowed his head. From what I could see, his lips were moving. Were his eyes closed, too? Sure enough, they were. I also bowed my head. Despite having no idea what he was asking for, I asked God to please answer Piper's prayers.

After he finished praying, the house screams were so deafening that I could not hear my own. I could tell from the soreness in my throat, though, that I was definitely yelling. Thanks to Raq I was here. Piper had stopped through Toledo once before since he'd started touring last year and—just like tonight—it was at an eighteen-and-up party. This never would have happened when I was friends with the Fan Five. They were probably dressed up in store-bought witch and cat costumes, sitting around in Jewel's basement with some lame boys from St. John's and drinking spiked punch.

A spotlight caught Piper's very first step as he began pacing the stage, and it chased his hyper moves as he bounced around, working every angle for the crowd.

> They said beats make the songs,
> so I made the song
> wit' da beat all wrong.
> Made your girl eye roll you
> throwin' me her thong . . .

Oh my goodness! And when the hook was near, Piper simply turned the microphone to the crowd. As if they'd been rehearsing for weeks, everyone sung the words. I, however, glanced over at Raq. Despite the sea of harmony blasting from the room, despite having heard Buckstarr—a reality show bimbo turned video groupie turned songster—sing the words so many times on the CD, in that moment, the only voice I heard, the only one that mattered, was Raq's.

> *It's Piper . . . It's Piper . . .*
> *He steps. He swags.*
> *He goes. You go . . .*
> *Follow-follow-follow-follow me.*
> *Followww . . . mee . . .*
> *He is . . . the Piper . . .*
> *Said, he is, the Piper . . .*
> *So do not forget.*
> *His fee . . .*

Piper pumped his fist in the air, loving every moment, exchanging dap with his hype men, a few of whom I now recognized from their profiles on the Underground Hip-Hop Web site where Raq and I both were members. Sure enough, there were Sir Gee and Cyn 21.

Turning the mic to the crowd again, Piper couldn't contain a laugh as the fans screamed through the chorus.

It's weird, the feeling you get when someone is staring at you, how most times you don't even realize that that's what the feeling is until you see the eyes on you.

I just knew that I felt . . . *something*.

So I looked back.

And our eyes locked.

Hitz.

He may have seemed soft, but was he?

Raq was bouncing to the beat, singing along, totally oblivious. But then she, too, must have sensed something because she turned and looked at me. I stood frozen and exaggerated a stare right back at her. She smacked her lips.

"Chica!" She laughed. "The hell is wrong with you? All this and you're just gonna stand there and lame out?"

"Hitz is backstage," I said. "You think he knows you clipped him?"

Her eyes grew instantly annoyed. "Piper is out there giving it and you're worried about that fool? Come. On. Kick it!"

Piper's anthem ended and he was now talking straight on to the crowd. The VFW, I bet, could hold about three hundred at most. That night, it sounded like thousands were out there screaming.

"Yo . . . y'all coulda been anywhere in the world tonight—"

His talking was interrupted by more cheers.

Raq was staring at me, her eyes dancing with a plea. *Forget Hitz. Be over that.*

Then she smiled playfully, visibly begging me to be excited with her.

It worked.

Yeah. *Forget Hitz.* That fool. Over there sulking about a backstage pass. Ha!

Piper continued, "But yo . . . Y'all chose to be with me—"

The crowd's reaction was better than a touchdown during Super Bowl.

"And for that," he said, "I owe y'all my life—"

The stage slammed into darkness. The speakers screamed with silence. Then, *pow!* One red spotlight focused on Piper. Frozen still, his head was down and his fist was in the air.

I was trying to calm myself, to feel the intense moment Piper was working so effortlessly to create, but the excitement made it impossible.

He waited a long time for silence, couldn't get it, and so, sans music, he began regardless.

> *Raised in the guttas, the block my mother*
> *Dope game my sista, fiends like my brothas*
> *Monsta it made me,*
> *Monsta money it gave me . . .*
> *Monstuuuuuuh . . .*

The beat kicked in, slow and melodic, some John Coltrane sample, and Piper flowed through "Monsta in the Mirror," his autobiographical ballad. Respectful, the crowd hung on every single word, didn't dare breathe during every bar of confessions. His lyrics were grim, full of grit and regret. Beautiful.

Unconsciously though, I guess I was wondering if we were still being watched. And so I turned my head.

Hitz was off to the side, his stolen VIP pass replaced now with a fresh one. His eyes were locked hot on Raq's backside.

I looked around, desperate to recall the way we'd come in, to find the corridor we'd walked through. But backstage was jam-packed now with all of the people concentrated in one area to watch the show, so it was nearly impossible to see the way out.

Finally, I spotted a neon red sign above a door. EXIT. A clique of groupies, repped strong and looking determined, were standing in front of it. Still, if push came to shoving past Hitz, I decided that we could get through them.

DJ Kindred was standing beside Hitz, making small talk, not realizing that Hitz was only halfheartedly responding with an occasional laugh and a quick look at him every once in a while. Then, something he said must have been funny because Hitz gave in and exchanged agreeable dap as they cracked up laughing. Thank *goodness* for DJ Kindred.

> *Raised by the streets, but God bless my mother*
> *Swift money my first love, Glock nine my other*
> *Monsta it made me,*

Monsta pain it gave me . . .

Monstuuuuuuh . . .

I nodded my head and rocked to the rhythm.

And I couldn't believe it.

Piper had touched me.

He'd called me—

He'd dubbed me—

Glitz.

No, I couldn't sing like Raq. If the two of us walked into a room, *she* would be noticed first. I'd have never had the nerve to steal someone's pass—or to steal anything, for that matter. Gramma would sense it and teleport herself in front of me to remind me what she taught me when I was just a little girl: "When you steal, eventually you'll be stolen from. It's wrong. And it's bad karma."

But if it weren't for that pass, I'd have only daydreamed of being backstage, of seeing Piper up so close. I nodded my head to the beat and this time felt my whole body moving as well. And no harm was even done—Hitz already had a new pass. Plus, *I* hadn't stolen anything. Technically.

¤ ▉ ¤

Immediately after Piper's concert, Raq grabbed the arm of Sir Gee, his number one hype man, as he and the other guys made their way past us backstage. Security was too close to Piper for her to reach him, but Sir Gee was accessible. A big, burly guy, he had a crunchy-looking beard and irritated eyes. He was the least attractive of the crew but because he was Piper's right-hand man, he was definitely important.

"I've been dying to meet you," Raq told Sir Gee, gently holding his arm.

I looked around. No sign of Hitz. Whew.

Sir Gee checked out the cutie before him, his eyes softening. "Word?"

"Yeah," Raq said. "You're, like, my favorite."

Sir Gee shouted ahead, "I'll catch up!" And the huddle of hype men and security that surrounded Piper continued on to the dressing room as Sir Gee turned back to Raq. "What's your name, ma?"

"Raquel." She put her hand out for him to shake.

Instead, Sir Gee turned her palm down and pulled her hand to his mouth. After kissing it, he said, "What's good, Raquel?"

Raq stepped in closer as he kissed her hand again. "My ex-boyfriend is lurking around back here and I don't feel like having no drama—"

Sir Gee backed away a step but still didn't let go of Raq's hand. "Ay, ma, I'm not tryna be dealin' with no drama either—"

"Please." Raq rolled her eyes. "I said *ex*. Some fools don't know how to push on, you know? But I do wanna kick it with you for a minute," she said, moving in to close the space between them once again.

For such a big guy, it was hilarious to see Sir Gee nearly blush.

In an effort to seal the deal, Raq went on telling Sir Gee about her "ex-boyfriend." "He used to beat me," she said. With her big brown eyes and sincere voice, she looked like a tiny damsel standing next to Sir Gee, a protective grizzly bear. "You know him, right? Hitz?"

He laughed. "Are you serious? That skeleton?" He frowned. Then he scratched his beard and laughed a nervous chuckle, wrinkles denting his dark skin. "Yo, he did that to you, ma?"

She sighed. "Crazy, huh? So that's why I'm just saying, you know . . . If he sees me talking to you he might . . . But I would like to kick it with you."

Sir Gee took his tenth glance at Raq's thick thighs and mature hips and sighed. Without another word, he nodded for us to follow and continued up the corridor, passing two dressing rooms before stopping in front of another. Once again Raq had worked it so we were positioned like we belonged. *Dudes are real stupid when you act like you're gonna put it on 'em*, Raq had once said.

Cyn 21, the pensive-looking member of Piper's crew, was standing by Piper's doorway like *he* was security. Shaking his head, he looked at Raq then at me. To Sir Gee, he said, "Let me holler at you, man," With a huff and a frown, he waited.

Sir Gee sniffed. "Later," he told Cyn 21. Then he took Raq's hand. "Come on, ma."

As if it were no big deal, like she'd *expected* this to work, Raq prepared to follow Sir Gee into Piper's dressing room and I stuck close behind them.

"You know, Pipe don't like no damn drama," Cyn 21 said.

"Won't be none," Raq chimed.

Sir Gee added, "Cyn . . . I got this, man." He began *knock-knock-knock*ing on the heavy metal door. "Yo! Yo!" he called until someone opened it.

Cyn 21 still looked peeved, but he just shrugged as we all went in. I glanced up at the digital clock next to the exit sign up ahead. A half hour until midnight.

No point in sweating it. No way was I making it home on time.

What was I supposed to say? *Raq, I know we're just about to get into Piper's dressing room, but I have to miss this once-in-a-lifetime opportunity so I can go home. Have fun without me.* No way!

I'd never missed curfew though.

Well, at least it'd be worth it.

What's Gramma gonna do? Punish me forever?

Piper's dressing room was minimally furnished and a bit disappointing. It was so bare and small—not at all what I imagined. The only light was a bulb hanging from the ceiling. *Where is the dressing table?* I wondered. *The vanity lights?*

On the far end of a sunken-in green couch, with a steaming wet white rag covering his eyes as he leaned back and chilled, was Piper.

He didn't even bother to look up as his other hype men and a small entourage of unfamiliar and forgettable faces—cats from the hood he was reppin' no doubt—exchanged dap with Sir Gee and Cyn 21 and crowded the room. I settled into position by a rickety-looking coatrack and watched Raq perform. I noticed that we were the only two girls in the room and I eyed the door just in case. The deadbolt was off. Good.

Raq was fluttering her arms around like an anxious butterfly, making exaggerated gestures as she laughed and joked around, keeping Sir Gee in her spell. Like she belonged.

Like she'd been here before. Like this was her show. Her destiny. Quietly I was proud of my friend. Look where she'd gotten us. My goodness. Backstage with Piper! And yet she was being so cool. I wished I could be like that, too.

Sir Gee cracked up at something she said, and when he leaned back, I noticed a digital clock on the wall behind him: 11:41.

I thought about borrowing Raq's phone and calling Gramma to tell her I was soon to be on my way home, that I was just going to be a little late. Then I remembered that there was no reasoning with her. No way would she have just said, "Okay, see you when you get here." Yeah right. I was better off to just deal with her fussing later. Why ruin my fun?

Some guy called out to Piper and he responded—without taking the rag off of his face—by nodding. Someone pushed a glass into his hand and Piper caressed it. Then he took a sip. I watched his wristband, snow white like the rest of his gear, and noticed his nails. Clean and well-filed.

The room was stuffy and it smelled liked cigars. It was hard to tell who had been smoking them, but I guessed it wasn't Piper. Unlike the average MC, Piper never once mentioned smoking *anything* in his rhymes. He was a straight fool, though, when it came to rhyming about his champagne.

> *Bump milk.*
> *Even mah mama knows . . .*
> *poured champagne on my Cheerios . . .*

Raq was playfully arguing with Sir Gee now. He'd just taken a sip of something in a cup and, teasingly, wouldn't let her taste it.

Sir Gee joked, "Ma, you talk more smack than a little bit. You know that, right?"

Maybe it was just the rush from the show, I don't know, but I felt electrified, like someone had plugged me in and I was working for once, like I'd been lying dormant for seventeen years. All the excitement of a million amusement parks, yet I couldn't bear to move and enjoy myself.

Raq, on the other hand, slid right into her biographical spiel. "I've been singing since I was born," she said to Sir Gee. "You better recognize . . ."

Piper looked from under his rag and checked out Raq with a glance, finally noticing her presence in the room. "Yo, who's shorty, man?"

"For real . . . " added Cyn 21, his face smug.

Sir Gee gave admiring eyes to Raq. "Tell 'em who you are, ma."

Piper covered his face again. "Looks like somebody's lookin' for trouble . . ."

Raq rolled her eyes. "Not tryna be nobody's girl toy, playa."

Everyone laughed, letting out resounding *oohs* and impressed *ahhhs*.

Even Piper had to chuckle.

"I'm just sayin'," Raq said. "My name is Raquel Marissa Diaz. But my stage name is Raq." She swiped the cup from an off-guard Sir Gee and took a sip. "Don't be gettin' nothing twisted up in here. Your boy Sir Gee is mad cool, but we just trying to hang."

Piper pulled the rag off of his face again and nodded. "All right. But yo . . . who is *we*?"

I picked something invisible off of my jeans, brushed a speck of glitter off my hoodie, and then stared down at my Pumas. I felt like a fool and I hoped I didn't look like one, too. I wanted to speak up, to say something, but I wasn't sure what. My gaze fell back on Piper. He was still looking from up under his rag. And now he was watching me.

"We," Raq said, "is me and my best friend over there."

They all looked at me then.

The new girl in the room who'd been there all along.

"Yo," Piper said. "Homegirl over there lookin kinda scared. Matter-a-fact, a li'l pet-tro-fied, you ask me. She think on delay or something?" They all hooted and hollered and I felt the heat of a million spotlights on my face.

Raq waited for the laughter to die off and, with perfect timing to sound completely unbothered, she offered, "Hardly, playa. My girl is mad cool."

Sir Gee chuckled. "Leave shorty alone. She over there mindin' her own."

I took a deep breath, my insides aching with nervousness. "It's all good," I said, purposefully looking right at Piper when I said it. "Just here to chill."

Piper shrugged. "Yo." He smiled that extra white smile. "So chill. Y'all cool."

Then, just that quick, Raq and Sir Gee were happily back into their flirtation and the other hype men in the room got back to chatting. My heart was thumping in my ears as I looked around trying to make myself relax. Me and Raq were the only two girls in a roomful of guys we'd only hoped to meet, and yet I'd always imagined us being side by side if it really happened. Instead, she was on the other side of the room fitting in, engaged in conversation, and I was sitting here looking corny.

Then I caught an unexpected glimpse of myself in a corner mirror across the room and the image smacked me back into reality. ARTIST had dripped down my face and appeared now like random splotches of glitter. The sparkle, though, was a reminder that I was Glitz—like Piper had called me—and that Glitz wouldn't be scared in a situation like this. Glitz would be working the room. Glitz would be totally at ease. And so it was settled. I had to stop being Ann Michelle. Immediately.

6

The door to Piper's dressing room flew open then, interrupting all the laughter and small talk, not to mention Raq's animated storytelling, and all the chaos of the backstage crowd flooded in as a short, pudgy guy peeked in. "Ready, Pipe?"

Piper raised his fist in the air. "Yo . . . ever since my mama said, '*My water just broke*,'" he replied to immediate laughter.

Just as the door closed, I made eye contact with a ticked-off-looking hoochie standing in the hall, who immediately scowled at the sight of me. "Ugh! I *know* that skinny chick ain't Piper's girl!"

Another random girl whose face I couldn't see sounded just as dejected. "He could do *so* much better."

Piper was too busy getting off of the couch to pay attention to what they'd said about me. He sat up, his knuckles cracking as he reached down to fix his shoes, no laces of course—Run-DMC was often mentioned in his rhymes and always traceable in his style. Then Piper hopped up and prepared to leave.

I glanced up at the clock—12:11

Raq finally came over to me. "Sir Gee said we can go eat with them."

I looked up at the clock again—12:12

An entire minute had passed that quick.

I was twelve minutes past curfew.

Raq was smiling at me. Waiting. Ecstatic. "You wanna go?" she asked.

Ann Michelle might have said no, but not Glitz.

I shrugged and smiled right back. "Of course," I said. "Are you nuts?"

"Yes!" She laughed. "And you must be, too, I take it. Your curfew . . ."

I shrugged. "I'm already late now."

She held her hand up for a high five. "My *chica . . .*"

Christmas. That would be the worst-case scenario. *You can't leave your room until Christmas.* That wouldn't be so bad, I told myself. Gramma wouldn't punish me past then, would she?

Once we were all ready to head out, Cyn 21 opened the door again.

A skinny-faced chicken was standing in the hallway, kicking it with hoochies. Sir Gee immediately peeped this and stood up a little straighter. He announced to me and Raq, "Y'all cool. Don't even sweat that dude. Y'all with me."

Before I knew it, we were whisked down the corridor—

forced into a tight formation with the crew— protected by the uniformed security that lined the halls and Piper's homeboy security that helped make up his entourage.

We exited the heavy metal door to the outside where several SUVs were running.

The cool air of the night slapped my face. It even *felt* late.

Piper crawled in to the open door of a black SUV first before Sir Gee got in. Somehow, I got in next. On instinct, I crawled back to the third row, where Piper was. Raq gave a shove to the small of my back but I ignored her. What was I supposed to do, sit next to Sir Gee so *she* could ride next to Piper? Whatever. She'd sewed herself close to Sir Gee all night. Why stop now?

Just as Cyn 21 hopped in the front seat next to the driver, someone locked the doors. My neck jerked as we hot peeled it out of the parking lot and I let out a nervous chuckle.

Piper kinda laughed, too. "Yo! I think my scalp just flew off," he joked. I tried to relax and laugh along with him, but my next sound came out sounding more like a cough.

I was sitting close enough to Piper to smell the minty-freshness of his gum. Meanwhile, Raq and Sir Gee were nestled close together in the middle row in front of us. Once again, Raq was talking nonstop. Unsure of what else to do with my hands, and not wanting Piper to see how raggedy my nails looked, I sat on them.

Piper yelled up front to our driver, "Ay yo, pimpin'! Too

quiet up in here." His dreads looked thicker up close than in pictures, almost like they were too heavy for his tiny face, but knowing he was Piper made him so fine to me.

A moment later, a slow jam banged from the speaker. It was an old cut by the Isley Brothers; I recognized the song as one of Gramma's favorites, and my heart rippled at the thought of her. I pushed away the heavy feeling as best as I could as we breezed onto I-475, trailed by the two other SUVs in Piper's entourage.

Piper stretched his hand out to me. "Yo, my apologies for not properly introducing myself. Piper . . ."

I took my hand out from beneath my lap to oblige his handshake. I couldn't believe it. As if he actually needed an introduction. His hand was a bit cold and his shake was firm.

"My friends call me Glitz," I said.

No one but Piper had ever called me that, of course, but from now on things were going to be different in my life. New name, new me. It made complete sense.

He nodded. "Yo . . . Glitz . . . You enjoy the show?"

I felt a smile on my face. "It was the best concert I've ever seen in my life."

Seeming pleasantly surprised, he said, "For real?"

I couldn't get rid of the stupid grin that had glued itself to my face.

He took a moment before he spoke again. "Yo . . . I'm

humbled by the gratification." His lips crawling into a smile, he said, "Only a fool would take that answer for granted. And Piper takes nothing for granted, ya dig?"

I nodded, slipping my hand back into the warmth underneath my thigh.

"I dig," I said.

"So, you listen to a lot of music?"

Still stuck in a grin, I said, "Yours."

He laughed. "That's what's up." Then he nodded to the groove that was playing. "You do like the Isley Brothers, too, though, right?"

"Yes."

Again, he chuckled. "Yo . . . you all right wit' me then, Glitz."

Glitz.

Wow.

"So yo . . . What you dig with Piper's music?"

Standing in a room trying to be cute and impress people and get guys' attention? *That* made me nervous. *That* was something I would probably never do as good as Raq. But chatting about music? *Piper's* music at that? Breezy.

I said, "Your lyrics. For one. You're always so clever. . . . And you're so smart."

His face was pensive, though I know he had to have heard that compliment before. "I appreciate that," he said.

I added, "And your delivery is just so cool. It's like your

words are just gonna have to speak for themselves. You're not anxious to prove you can flow. You don't shout over the tracks. You don't change your pitch when you get to the best rhyme. It's like . . ." I noticed the impressed smile on his face and I stopped talking.

He laughed quietly and turned his face toward the window, watched the traffic for a few moments, then mumbled the rhyme, "*Asking her the questions, then I cold collect. Such humbling words from Glitz . . . the intellect.*"

Double wow.

He looked back at me. "Piper appreciates that, yo . . ."

My heart at ease, I continued with confidence, "And I really love, too, how you'll pick a wild track, something unpredictable, like heavy acoustic, and sound just as hot as you do on a Beatz Boys track. It's like you don't *have* to have bass to be comfortable, you know? I bet you could rhyme over a country track and it'd still be hype."

He laughed. "Yo . . . I like you."

I found myself laughing right along with him, totally comfortable this time.

He said, "You really do love music, huh?"

"Oh my goodness," I said. "A *lot.*"

All of a sudden, Sir Gee shouted into his phone. "Man, look! Tell Mun I said we'll be there. Just keep the AC on in the room so it's cool up in there when Pipe walks through the door. Feel me? We gonna grab some grub and keep pushing up the e-way."

Piper leaned in and whispered to me then. "Don't mind him. He's just very hungry."

We both laughed.

Piper closed his eyes and nodded a gracious nod. His eyes closed, he seemed to be talking to no one in particular, mumbling "Yo . . . *She loves Piper's music, Piper wonders why. Why love Piper's music . . .*" He shook his head, scrunched up his eyebrows and kept mumbling other things.

He opened his eyes, looked inquisitively at the ceiling, and then closed them again. *"Thankful."* Then he said, "You love Piper's music, means you gotta love me. Because yo . . . My music? All any of it really is, *is* my life."

He opened his eyes and looked at me. He said. "Ya dig?"

I nodded. "I do."

Raq peeked over her shoulder to glance back at me. Piper's knuckles were touching my knee and Raq noticed this just as Sir Gee's arm pulled her closer. She yelled over the music, her loudness seeming out of place with how mellow Piper was now.

"What up, my *chica*?" Raq's voice sounded like she was having the time of her life. She'd gotten us here and she seemed more than proud.

Piper chuckled and said to me. "Yo . . . your girl is a lively one." And then, his voice was a bit quieter, he said, "But y'all seem cool as a fan . . . Real cool. . . ."

He leaned back, nestled his head into a comfortable-looking position, and fell asleep. There was a moment of silence as the music changed to a Shirley Murdock song. Piper's knuckles were warm on my knee, and I felt calm inside as I listened to the soft, steady sounds of his breathing. I'd never heard anyone breathe as nice as him.

He turned his face toward mine and his breathing was weighty on my neck. Eventually he would awake and I would wake up, too, from this crazy night that was so amazing it must be a dream. For now, though, I watched him sleep. The girl with glitter melting down her face. The girl who sported backpacks instead of purses, whose fingernails were stubby. The Fan Five outcast. I was here.

Maybe time wasn't on my side. Maybe the carriage would eventually turn back into a pumpkin, the horses into mice, but for now it was real. *So* real.

⬦ ⬥ ⬦

The bright yellow lights of the Waffle House screamed, instantly waking everyone as we pulled into the parking lot. The driver turned off the ignition and the sudden lack of music made the silence too loud. I recognized where we were—this was the Waffle House in the Central Avenue strip mall—and calculated that we were about twenty minutes from home. I, too, had dozed off. What time was it now? A part of me didn't even want to know. If only I were grown and free, I wouldn't have to worry about such things.

As Piper's entourage unloaded from the three SUVs, I followed Raq into the bathroom. Sir Gee, Piper, and everyone else grabbed tables.

Because there was only one toilet and I didn't have to go, I washed my hands while Raq took a squat. She tossed me some gloss and laughed real loud. "My *chica!*" She screamed with excitement. "You wanna believe this?"

Shaking my head in disbelief, I could only smile. "All because of you!"

"I'm gonna be in with Piper," she said. "I'm so freakin' close!"

"I can't believe I was actually sitting next to him," I said.

"Oh, and Greg says we can come with them to Detroit, sit in at the studio," she sounded even more ecstatic.

"Greg?" I asked.

"That's Sir Gee's real name," Raq told me. *Interesting*, I thought. Now she and Gee were on a first-name basis.

"So we can really go with them to the studio?" I asked. "When?" I was already wondering how I'd get off of the punishment I was sure to get from Gramma so I could go along. I'd never tried to sneak out the window, but hey, there was a first time for anything.

"Now!" Raq said. "Tonight. After we eat. Detroit is just fifty minutes away. Well, with dude driving, make that like twenty minutes away." She laughed.

"Tonight?"

"You know how we read about it, how they stay up in the studio all night? How Piper's always posting updates online saying, *'Yo. Piper just got in. Been putting genius to tracks,'* at like six, seven o'clock in the morning?"

What she was saying was true. We had read about how Piper and a lot of people in the music industry stay up all night recording.

She said. "So what up, *chica*? You wit' it?"

"What time is it?" I asked.

She whipped out her phone. "One twenty-two—"

"Are you serious?" It took all the determination I had to not look over at Raq, who was still sitting on the toilet. I stared wide-eyed at my own reflection as I used a wet paper towel to wipe the remaining remnants of glitter off my cheek. I shrugged. "Well, I'm definitely going to be grounded through Christmas, and I guess I can forget about spring break, too."

I had made my peace with being a few hours late for curfew, but coming home the next morning? That was another thing altogether. There was no way I could go all the way to Detroit in the middle of the night with a bunch of rappers and not have my grandmother lock me away for the rest of my natural-born life.

But how could I get out of it now? It wasn't like I could ask Piper's driver to drop me off at home on the way to the studio. Maybe that was something Ann Michelle would have done, but not Glitz.

"Motor City Soundz," Raq shouted the name of Mun-E's famous studio as she flushed. "Here we come!"

I stepped back from the mirror so Raq could slip in front of me and wash her hands.

She started fixing her makeup—which was actually still pretty flawless—and said, "Mun-E's even gonna be there!"

If I'm dreaming, I thought, *please don't wake me up.*

I screamed. "Yes!"

She screamed, too. "Yeah, *chica.* Tonight is our Jack. Pot."

Mun-E was Piper's manager, known around as one of hip-hop's up-and-coming heavyweights. When Raq and I had imagined her making it, we'd said things like, "We gotta meet Mun-E someday." But who would have imagined we actually *would*?

"Raq," I said, "this is too good to be real!"

"I know." She laughed. "But I was sitting right there when Mun's assistant called Gee. You probably thought I was pushed all up on him 'cause I was digging him, right? Please. I'm just trying to stay in close, you know? I'm trying to do this thing for real, *chica.* This ain't just a dream. It's my life!"

Still in awe, I said, "So Gee said he's gonna introduce you to Mun-E?"

"Noooo . . ." She laughed. "But he said Mun was going to be in the studio tonight. *I* said I'm going to meet him. Are you crazy? You think I'd go all the way to Detroit, be in the same room, and *not* bless him with my voice? That's Mun-E, *chica*. That's money!"

"Yeah." I laughed. "Oh my goodness . . ." I leaned back and used the wall to brace myself. "Okay. But how will I get home? And when?"

"Trust me, you'll get back. First thing in the morning," Raq assured me with a wink. "So, you wit' it?"

I didn't answer right away.

I was contemplating what in the world I would tell Gramma.

Then Raq said, "By the way, I peeped you all close up with Piper. So I *know* you're not trippin' too much."

I fought hard not to grin. Maybe Raq *wasn't* mad at me for riding close to Piper. When she'd pushed me in the small of my back when I'd gotten in first and rode next to him, I thought she had wanted that seat for herself. Now I was thinking that maybe her shove was because she was excited for me.

Raq tilted her head as she looked at me in the mirror. Then she gave me a sharp, quick nudge. "Check it," she said. "And listen close, all right? Because I'm serious when I say this. Those people back home, as far as me, I'm just extra income and a way for them to feel good about themselves, the grown-up Girl Scout and the grown-up Boy Scout, you know? I'm like just some extra gesture they did for society. So they can say they kept some bad-assed girl out of juvie and sent her to a college prep school instead."

I nodded. When Raq had first told me about her foster parents, I thought what they were doing for her was kind of cool. But maybe she was right—maybe what they were doing for her was more for themselves than it was for Raq. Maybe they really *were* just phony parents.

She said, "So you think I'm gonna pass tonight up for *them*? You think I'm thinking twice about rolling with Greg tonight? Roll up to the D so maybe I can have a shot doing what *I* want to do? Sure, I could go back to Judge and Kitty tonight, go to bed and wake up tomorrow to her corny-ass pancakes and syrup . . . and all that phoniness. But for what?"

I was feeling more and more empowered as she continued, "Stackin' dollars and livin' fab starts tonight, *chica*! So don't trip on your grandmother. You can't keep living your life for her, laying bricks for a house *she* wants you living in. This is your time to do what *you* wanna do!"

With that, I held my hand for Raq's cell phone.

Gramma snatched up the phone on the first ring. "Where. Are. You?" she demanded without even hearing my voice first to confirm it was me. "And why didn't you take your phone? I call you and some song about a monster keeps blasting from your room!"

I sighed, asking God real quick in my mind to forgive me for the lie I was about to tell. I'd never been seriously dishonest with Gramma before—for fear of God giving her the instincts to recognize that I was—so I asked Him to be on my side, just this once.

I said, "I wanted to call you earlier but I forgot my phone. And, um, Raq's couldn't keep a signal or something. Her battery . . . We caught a flat. Had to walk to her house. I'll—"

"Didn't I tell you that little demon child was bad luck. Didn't I? Huh? That tire was a sign! Going *nowhere*, I told ya!"

"People get flat tires all the time," I told Gramma. "Listen, we're both exhausted. Plus, I have a headache. Plus, my feet are beat up from walking. I'm just gonna crash here, okay? Be home tomorrow? First thing." I held my breath, grimaced, and waited for the heat of her wrath to escape from the speaker.

But Raq snatched the phone. "Hi, Gramma! It's me . . . Raquel. Listen, it's totally my fault. I thought I had juice on my phone and didn't—" Raq held the phone away from her face as Gramma yelled something—a bunch of things—that I couldn't make out.

Raq said, "Yes, yes . . . I know. I know you were worried . . . Yes . . . Well, no ma'am . . . I . . . The devil? No I don't worship . . . No . . . Well, I just want you to know that we're *okay*. Okay?

Hopefully it's all right with you she can just crash here. . . ."
With an offended look on her face—no doubt due to something
Gramma had said to her—Raq handed me back the phone.

She turned back to the mirror and said nothing while she
fixed herself up.

"Gramma?" I said.

"*First* thing in the morning you'd better be home. You hear
me? I knew I shouldn't have taken my sinus pill. If I didn't think
I would end up driving on somebody's sidewalk, I'd get in my
car right now and snatch you up! Do you have a toothbrush to
use? Do they have clean pajamas for you to borrow?"

"Yes, Gramma."

"All right now. Better floss, too. No telling how much candy
you been eating today. And don't forget to—"

I wanted to scream! Sixteen years old and she was telling
me to brush and floss my teeth! "Okay, Gramma," I replied.
"I'll see you in the morning." I think she was still talking when
I hung up.

Sir Gee's back was to us, and he was sitting directly across from Piper and Cyn 21 in the Waffle House booth. Gee was so much larger than Piper—and even Cyn 21—that he looked like their bodyguard. They were all leaned in and looking tense. I tried to make eye contact with Piper, but he was too focused in on what Sir Gee was saying to notice us approaching.

I slid in beside Piper, forcing Cyn 21 to move over even more, which made him clear his throat with irritation. Raq sat next to Gee.

"One thing I can't stand," Sir Gee was saying, "is a man that'd put his hands on a woman. Gets me *irked*."

"Yo . . ." Piper nodded. "It's atrocious."

Sir Gee sighed into a smile when he looked at Raq. "We was just discussing your mans . . ."

"Oh," Raq replied, looking impressively unfazed. "Forget that jerk."

"Yeah," Gee confirmed. "Got a call from Muns. He got word that Hitz is going around looking for 'the Latina chick backstage, the one with Sir Gee.' Said he saw her leavin' with us. Said when he find her, it's on. Skinny fool don't know who he's dealin' wit', ma. Muns is crazy. And my deck ain't too damn full either, ya dig? And don't *none* of us like a punk."

"Yo . . ." Piper said, "Any man that puts his hands on a female? Straight—"

"*Punk!*" Gee finished Piper's statement.

Everyone laughed.

And Raq shrugged. "Told you he was crazy." She swallowed. "What else did Mun-E say?"

Gee shrugged. "I just told him, I said, '*Look* man, homey is just a skinny-assed punk.' I told him all about Hitz and his dirty paws. Ain't nobody tryna entertain a punk like that, some skinny dude on some simple shit, reppin' Toledo cats all wrong."

Raq said, "Fools stupid like that in Detroit, too. Don't get it twisted."

Gee nodded. "But callin' Mun-E lookin' for you?" He shook his head with a *tsk-tsk.* "So ill . . ."

Piper said, "Yo . . . Not trying to say—you know—that a woof-face necessarily deserves a beat down, but you too gorgeous for bruises, girl."

Looking flattered, Raq turned her head toward Piper and smiled. "Thank you," she said.

It was no surprise that even Piper noticed her beauty. Raq's eyes dazzled when she spoke and her smile was electric. Of *course* he thought she was beautiful. But I can't deny how it made me feel. Not jealous, no. Well, okay, maybe just a little, but she already had Gee all googly-eyed over there. Jeez.

Cyn 21 finally spoke up, his voice dry, "So how long he been hittin' you?"

Raq's eyes fluttered with annoyance at Cyn 21's probing. "*Too* long," she said. "But actually, I hate even talking about it. It's so embarrassing."

Sir Gee looked over at me. "How long your girl been getting beat up by her mans?"

I shrugged, glancing over at the table across from us where other members of Piper's entourage were having their order taken by the waitress. I said, "They're not together, now. So it's all good."

"Right. But how long?" Cyn pressed.

What is up with this dude?

Cyn 21 had like a big old chunk, not even a chip, on his shoulder, about something.

About what?

"Too long," I replied. And instantly I regretted doing so.

Already, within an hour, I'd told two lies. I didn't even know Hitz. He was probably harmless.

But just like that, Raq's lies had become mine.

Sir Gee looked disgusted by my answer, his nose scrunched up like something smelled in the room, "Any man that would hit a woman . . ." He frowned like someone had poured a mound of garbage on our table. "Disgusts me," he said.

Piper added, "Yo . . . First time I saw my stepdaddy hit my mama . . ." He shook his head.

> *Wasn't my daddy. Wasn't my blood.*
> *But I said okay, today, still thank you God.*
> *'Cause in our house. . . . there's still a man.*
> *But wasn't my daddy. Damn sure no blood.*
> *. . . why I said okay, today gotta warn you God.*
> *He hit my mama, so I cock aimed and shot . . .*

"That's one of my favorite songs," I said.

Piper looked perplexed. "What song?"

I realized then that the music had only been playing in my mind. Piper hadn't been rapping.

"'Wasn't My Daddy,'" I replied.

Piper nodded. "Yo . . ." He smiled. "That's what's up."

"Yeah," I said. "It's like I never ever wanted to kill anybody—never would or will—but you made me understand why you considered it, you know? And the way you rode the track, right ahead of the beat . . . it made me feel like you were on the run, like those nightmares you had about wanting to hurt your stepfather were literally chasing you—"

That's when I noticed that I had everyone's attention, even Cyn 21's. Sir Gee looked a little shocked—it was the most he'd heard me say all night—and Piper appeared, as usual, interested in what was on my mind.

Cyn 21 nodded. "Shorty's dope," he said.

"Yo . . ." Piper laughed and said to Sir Gee, "Told you, man."

Told him? Told him *what*? Had he really told them about our conversation in the car?

"How old are y'all?" Cyn 21 wanted to know, eyeing me real quick. "Y'all look young."

"Grown," Raq immediately replied. "That's how old."

"Yo," Piper said. "Better be."

A red-haired waitress interrupted us. "What can I getcha?"

◻ ◼ ◻

Soon, we were slamming on scrambled eggs with cheese, hash browns, fat juicy steaks, and toast, and the two waitresses on duty were working hard to keep everyone happy. "More jelly? Need ketchup?" We were so busy eating and laughing that it didn't seem like much of a big deal at all that no one ever asked for a more specific answer about our ages.

Bzzzzz . . . Bzzzzz . . . Bzzzz . . . Sir Gee's cell phone was vibrating on the table and eventually bumped up against the side of his plate, which made the noise even more obnoxiously loud. *Bzzzz-clink . . . Bzzz-clink . . . Bzzzz-clink . . .*

"Yo." Piper took a sip from his orange juice. "Pick it up, my mans. Tell Mun we'll be there."

Sir Gee took a deep breath before answering, "Mun-E! We're on our way now. Half hour."

Raq popped the last bite of sausage into her mouth and listened in on Sir Gee's conversation. Piper leaned in and whispered in my ear. I had just raised my glass of ice water with lemon to my lips and began to sip when his whisper began.

"Yo," he said, "your girl? She'll be all right. Don't worry. Piper's gonna haveta show her some real love." Then, he went back to his orange juice.

He said that to me. And then he just *went back to his orange juice.*

Raq was watching us. She'd seen Piper whisper to me but she couldn't have heard what he'd said. She had Sir Gee next to her, obviously digging her, and now even Piper, next to me, was eyeing her, too. Me? Oh they liked that I knew something about good music, but that was it. I couldn't be wanted, too?

"I can't get there no faster than the man can drive," Sir Gee shouted into the phone. "See you when we get there!" He stuffed his phone into his pocket and attacked what was left on his plate.

Piper nudged me, then whispered a joke, "Gee's gonna have heartburn."

I forced my lips to curl up into a smile. Ha. Ha. He.

I felt so silly. When had delusions of possibility crept into my head in the first place? Just because I'd gotten to ride next to him, just because he'd actually had a conversation with me, just because he'd seemed impressed by all the things I'd said, I'd thought I had a chance with Piper? Please. Of *course* he would rather have Raq. Who was I kidding? And the worst part was that I couldn't blame him at all.

8

It was 3:37 in the morning when we finally got to the studio. Normally, driving from Toledo across the Michigan line to get to Detroit takes like an hour. Not tonight.

Mun-E was dumpy, bald, out of breath, and—at least now—so mad that spit was accompanying his every syllable. "Give me one reason, just anything"—he paced the lobby of the recording studio—"why I shouldn't be upset." He walked back and forth some more, grumbling before barking some more. "Time and paper just wastin' away while y'all somewhere stuffing your mouths! Coulda swore I said to be here *immediately* after the show."

For the longest, word on all the blogs was that Mun-E would sell his soul to go down in history as the Berry Gordy of hip-hop. He wanted Detroit to have not one but two famous music company pioneers. Ever since he'd taken over Motor City Soundz, Mun-E had been working to crank out hip-hop classics the way Hitsville/Motown had done for R&B.

And it was no secret that Piper was to be Mun-E's claim to legendary status.

Funny. Out of all the books I'd read about Motown— Gramma's shelves were stocked full—I never got the impression that Mr. Gordy would have ever yelled at Smokey Robinson, Stevie Wonder, or the Supremes.

Shoot.

Gramma.

Don't. Think. About. Gramma.

Motor City Soundz sat in the pit of the inner city, a forgotten street off of 8 Mile Road. It looked like any other plain, boring building where nothing exciting ever happened, but really it was the most happening place in hip-hop. Me, Raq, Piper, Cyn 21, and the rest of the entourage stood silent in the lobby, yet it seemed only I was nervous.

But from the bored expressions on everyone else's faces, these types of rants from Mun-E were routine. I knew from reading about Piper and his crew that they were all in their mid-twenties (Piper was twenty-three), and yet suddenly Mun-E (who I had read was around thirty-five) was acting like the only adult in a room full of children.

Sir Gee's booming voice was an instant reminder to everyone that he was no punk. "You don't see me standin' right here? Piper right in front of you? Look, we here, all right?"

"Yo . . ." Piper took time to choose his words, "Mun, my apologies."

Mun-E swallowed hard before turning his head away from Sir Gee to look directly at Piper. In a calmer voice, he said, "Nice job tonight, Pipe." But he might as well have said *Today is Saturday,* his tone was so unenthused. Then, in an even more eased-down voice, he addressed the entire entourage.

"Fellas, really. How many times I gotta tell y'all I don't give a damn how good you *were*? If it was five minutes ago or five years ago, it's in the past. Y'all waste time, you also waste my money. How good you gonna *be*. That's what's got to be your focus. Not *wanna be*. Not *was*. How good you *gonna be?* That's what the hell I care about."

Sir Gee rolled his eyes and sighed. "Mun, all we did was eat, man. That's it. We was hungry. We didn't even—"

Mun-E looked appalled and then laughed. "Eat? Y'all talking about eating?" An eerily excessive hooting erupted from his gut. "That shit is hilarious to me! Y'all got time to think about your stomachs? About *food?*" He laughed some more. Then a furious expression washed over his face. "We got hit records to make! Dollars to stack. Mansions to buy. For me, *islands* to buy. Platinum roads to build . . . Got more shows to tackle. And y'all worried about *food*? What the—?" Mun-E's eyes raced around the room in a rage before zeroing in on me. And then Raq.

"And who the hell's babysitting these two?" he asked.

The man was straight cuckoo, but Raq was gazing at him like he was King of Platinum Land just stepped off of his throne to address us.

Sir Gee was speaking through clenched teeth at this point, "Mun, I told you on the phone we had a couple of good friends with us. Let us in the booth already, man."

Mun-E sucked his teeth and then, with his nostrils flared, abruptly said, "We got time for the Buckstarr joint tonight and that's it. Let's knock that out real quick. Also, I just got y'all a few gigs on the road. Leavin' out tomorrow. The rest of y'all? Dismissed." He laughed a dry laugh and left the room.

Cyn 21 offered a loud grunt of disappointment. What was *up* with that guy?

"Yo." Piper spoke to his entire entourage but looked directly at Cyn 21. "Let's just give thanks to God for the blessing of a superior show this evening, ya dig? And for the fans that came out to support. Be thankful for the grace of safe travels, for the nourishment in our bodies, for the promise of what's yet to be seen."

The heaviness of the room lifted a bit, and Cyn 21 took a breath and relented. "Kill the booth, tonight, Pipe," he said. With that, he and the other two offered dap and quick hugs to Piper.

To Sir Gee, Cyn 21 said, "Can I holler at you, Gee?"

Gee replied, "You heard the man. I got the booth with Pipe."

Cyn 21 gave a blank stare as reply. "Won't take but a second."

"Hit you up in the A.M.," Sir Gee said.

"It's like that?"

Sir Gee sighed. "Me and Pipe gotta lay this track down."

I noticed Cyn 21 give Sir Gee a look. Icy.

Immediately, Sir Gee said, "Cool out, man. Real talk. In the A.M. . . ."

Cyn offered a stiff head-nod in return. "Yeah," he said. "A'ight then." He gave Piper dap, which eventually the entire entourage did again as they left.

As the lobby emptied out, Piper did a few neck rolls and stretched his arms.

He looked at Raq. "Ever been in a studio?"

"Nope," Raq answered. "And it feels good to be home!" She laughed.

Sir Gee chuckled. "Dame wants to get in that booth like she wants her next breath."

"That's right." Raq smiled. "Better ask about me."

"Yo," Piper said. "Mun's probably not in the best mood for experimentation tonight. Y'all are cool to come in and chill, but . . . I'm sure you understand."

Raq's face was blank. Then she looked at Sir Gee.

He shrugged. "All I said was *maybe*. You heard the man.

Might as well come witness the flow, though. You're here."

A flash of irritation crossed Raq's face. She was actually *disappointed* that she wasn't going to sing in front of Mun-E tonight? As irate as he'd been? How could she have even thought it was a possibility after that? My girl was certified delusional as far as I was concerned.

Sir Gee nodded at the door leading back into the studio. "Let's do this, Pipe."

Raq looked at me, her eyes excited regardless, and I could tell she'd already recovered from the let-down. Or at least she was doing a good job of pretending. "Let's roll, *chica*."

⊐ ◼ ⊐

Immediately, I was cold. The air conditioner had to be set on North Pole, it was so freezing in there. I was standing in the doorway of an overcrowded studio swollen with producers and tough-looking guys. Conversations had adjusted to a hush when Piper entered the room. I zipped my hoodie just as I realized that this was the very room where Swift-Katt, a would-have-been rap star from Detroit, had been gunned down last year.

Rumor had it that it was all the result of a middle-of-the-night scuffle over the absence of cheese on his burger and that Mun-E ordered the bullet to be fired by one of his men. Now Swift-Katt walks with a limp and has given up recording. I read that Mun-E had put a grip of money behind Swift-Katt, too, just like he did for Piper. Maybe that's why he's so serious now, like he'll be damned if he loses another investment over some foolishness. Piper was his plan B turned plan A.

I glanced at the clock on the wall—3:51.

In the wee hours of the night—when normally I would be asleep—these studio rats were wide-awake like it was two o'clock in the afternoon. I took mental attendance. Three guys were intent on finishing up a card game, four were holding cell phone conversations—all of which sounded like arguments— and Mun-E was sitting in front of the sound boards and audio controls with a bored expression on his face as he incessantly tapped a pencil on his knee, waiting.

There was a female in the room, too.

Sitting atop a monitor in the corner, she had an impossibly long jet-black weave and was wearing too much makeup, silk black leggings, and a fitted lace blouse. She eyed Raq and then noticed me, looking totally amused at the sight of both of us: two little wannabe fly girls who had *nothing* on her. Even with all the added hair since the last time I'd seen her on the dating reality show *Love Flava,* I recognized the attitude. Buckstarr.

I'd heard Mun-E mention her name, but it hadn't occurred to me that she was actually going to be there.

Her shimmery red lips produced a big fat pink bubble and she popped it loud. Known for her banging body, soprano voice, and raunchy lyrics, Buckstarr was on minute ten of her fifteen minutes of fame. I'd read the buzz about her on several gossip Web sites lately, how she'd been hired to harmonize hooks on a few of Piper's songs. I knew she had a decent voice from the season finale of the show, when she'd dramatically sung "And I Am Telling You, I'm Not Going . . ."—the theme song from *Dreamgirls*—as the show's security carried her off the set, kicking and crying. What made that last episode so memorable wasn't seeing the bachelor guy elope with his pick, it was the shot of Buckstarr after the commercial break. There had been a close-up of her—eyes completely dry of crocodile tears now—promising America that it wasn't the last time we were going to hear from her.

"Yo." Piper unzipped his jacket. "Kill the air now?"

Buckstarr hit a switch and a previously subliminal hum was silenced. She hopped off the monitor, at which point I noticed she was about seven inches taller than Piper because of her patent-leather stiletto boots. Then she followed him into the booth.

"Ay, Glitz," Sir Gee called back to me before going in, too, "step all the way in the room? Let the door close."

I kicked out the doorstopper and joined Raq on a velvet cushiony bench. The door snapped shut and someone dimmed the lights. Simultaneously, the inside of the booth lit up. It was wood paneled with two impressive-looking microphones inside. Piper, Buckstarr, and Sir Gee reappeared on the other side of the glass. Like magic.

Raq whispered under her breath, "Who's Glitz?"

Quietly, I murmured right back, "Me."

"Word?"

"Just roll with it."

She chuckled. "Alrighty, then. . . ."

I looked cautiously around and hoped that no one would tell me and Raq to leave now that Sir Gee—our advocate—was locked away in the soundproof booth. I breathed slowly. *Please don't let Mun-E's big fat Milk Dud head turn back around.*

High-pitched feedback screeched from the speakers as Piper, Buckstarr, and Sir Gee settled into headphones and adjusted the mics. Piper was on the right mic while Buckstarr and Sir Gee shared the other.

Mun-E slapped a button and, with utter disgust in his voice said, "All right. Let's get it!" What a beast. But there was something about him that commanded respect. Suddenly, even *I* wanted to impress him.

One of the sound guys said to the other, "Roll the track?"

The melody was so soulful, it reminded me of something funky and spellbinding that Gram—*don't say her name*—had played before, something from the seventies. A couple of seconds later I realized it was just that indeed. The beat was a sample from the Teena Marie and Rick James song

"Fire and Desire." I recognized it despite the tempo being sped up a bit. Buckstarr started humming, her soprano voice commanding every person in the room to look at her. Sir Gee watched her get into her groove like he was a hungry bulldog—licking his chops—and she was a juicy T-bone.

Riffing off the original, she sang, *"Ooooohhhh . . . A liar I desire . . . Set my heart on fire . . . I lovvvve you . . . Oh yeah."*

I peeped the new expression on Raq's face. *Damn, that should be me*, she was probably thinking. This made me wonder how the song would've sounded if it *had* been Raq on the track. Buckstarr's voice was real high-pitched, whereas Raq's was heavy and gutsy, full of soul. Buckstarr sounded pretty, no doubt about that, but Raq's voice was more powerful. Buckstarr's voice was cute, but Raq's was for real. Raq had a way of making you feel what she was singing about. And in an actual studio? *With* Piper? Man, she'd have rocked that song if given the chance to do so.

Piper jerked a braid away from his face and stepped closer to the microphone.

> *Look ma.*
> *Don't wanna make you cry, that's why,*
> *can't help myself—I gotta lie.*
> *Can't stand, it's so hard, seein' you sad.*

Other girls wanna be you bad. And when I'm alone on
*   this road*
and I'm wishing it was me you had,
I grab the next plump ass and they be girls gone mad.
Don't wanna let our love thing die.
But if I give you the truth, I kiss my piece, your mind
*   good-bye.*

Then he spoke the last bar.

See girl . . .
Yo . . .
I love you, too, but . . .
That why Pipe's gotta lie . . .

Sir Gee was chasing every one of Piper's rhymes with a
baritone echo, and the sound was so haunting it should have
been illegal. Piper's *"Lie,"* was chased by Sir Gee's, *"i-i-i . . ."*
Then Buckstarr would come back in . . .

Ooooohhhh . . . A liar I desire . . .
Set my heart on fire . . .
I lovvvve you . . . Oh yeah.

I looked at Raq and saw that glare was still in her eyes.
"You sound way better than her," I said. *"Any day."*

She smacked her lips. "Look better than her, too. Stank ho. While she's all up on my man . . ."

I wanted to laugh at her reaction but didn't for fear of Mun-E turning around. Instead, I just smiled. At least she'd referred to Sir Gee as her man and not Piper.

Buckstarr backed into Sir Gee, who—unlike Piper—was taller than she was. Sir Gee grabbed Buckstarr by her tiny waist and pulled her even closer.

Raq had it all. Looks. Body. Talent. Determination. Personality. Courage. No *way* could I stand to see her beat by a video vixen.

"Don't sweat it," I reminded her. Clearly, we'd just witnessed the recording of something really special, but for some reason that made me feel even more determined for Raq. She would record a song one day too, and I knew it. One day soon.

Raq side-eyed me and blew on her fingernails like she was sitting in a salon after having a manicure and smiled. "Just waiting my turn, *chica*."

9

Gramma would've taken one look at where we went after the recording was finished, and she would have declared it all a postcard from the devil.

She'd have fainted, too, to see me so gleefully walk in.

It was five o'clock in the morning and we had just pulled up to Sir Gee's crib on Livernois Avenue in Detroit. I could see through the window that the place was full of folks chilling as though it was mid-afternoon. It was like a *Tales from the Streets* movie or some gangster rap video that was being filmed on location. Only this was real. And I wasn't just some extra on a set. I was *invited* to be here . . . in actual life. It was the sweetest thing I'd ever imagined.

The music in the SUV had been so loud on the way over I could only tell that Raq and Sir Gee were talking a lot, but I couldn't hear any of what they were saying. As soon as we'd pulled away from the studio, Piper had slipped into a catnap while the driver whisked us over to Gee's house. Mostly, I'd just focused on hoping we'd get wherever we were going without crashing. I had imagined a mansion, something worthy of the Music Entertainment channel's *Pimped-Out Homes,* but we ripped through an alley and pulled up at the back fence of a simple two-story house in need of a paint job. The driver waited on the four of us to climb out before peeling back out of the driveway.

I had told Gramma I'd be home first thing in the morning. First thing was coming up pretty soon. As I watched the SUV pull away, the thought occurred to me that I could have banged on the window and asked for a ride home. But I knew the night wasn't over yet. More was going to happen. And I didn't want to miss it.

"Welcome to our humble abode." Sir Gee's voice was so loud and deep. He led us in through the back door and said, "Watch your step." We walked through the old-fashioned and messy kitchen. On top of the table—which was surrounded by chairs that did not match—were greasy pizza boxes, empty cans of root beer, and empty cans of regular beer, too. There were half-eaten bags of Hot Cheetos and Cool Ranch Doritos and a plastic pumpkin holding a few mini bags of Sugar Babies.

"Don't mind my homies," Gee said before swiping a brew from the counter and leading us up the hallway. I could hear the voices of people laughing in the next room and the sound of things crashing together followed by cheers. "My sister had a little Halloween set," he said. *Does Piper live here, too?* I wondered. I heard him yawn as our footsteps sounded against the hardwood floors.

Up ahead I could see the foyer, the dining room, and a gigantic front door. There was a front porch, too, full of lively people. Real people doing real things. Real life. The real world. Finally. *Ch-yeah . . .*

Guys with gold grills on their teeth nodded their approval as we entered the dining room. Instead of a table to eat at, there was a pool table. Someone took a shot, the balls clanked, and I realized that was the crashing sound I had heard on my way in.

A few guys were shooting dice in the corner, and the one who spotted Raq first started whistling. She strutted a little harder when they did, showing off her butt.

Sir Gee chuckled and called to his friends, "Don't act like y'all ain't never seen a sexy young woman before."

The dining room was connected to the living room. In there, four girls—looking unnecessarily sexy and excessively dolled-up for a house party—were sitting around watching *America's Funniest Home Videos* on the flat screen. You couldn't hear the TV, though, because the stereo was pumping Piper. Everyone was nodding their heads to the bass while they laughed at the screen.

"What up?" Sir Gee asked them.

"Hey," one said, though she didn't turn to look at him and no one seemed excited that Piper had just walked into the room. What would that be like, for seeing Piper to just be an everyday kind of thing? I couldn't imagine.

"Hey, Piper," said another.

"Yo . . ." Piper kicked back on a beat-up La-Z-Boy and looked up. "Y'all good?"

Sir Gee turned to Raq and me, then headed toward the steps that led to the second floor of the house. "Make yourselves comfortable," he said before walking up the creaky stairs, the faint *pop-pop* and then *fizzzz* of the opening can fading as he got farther away. "Be right back," he called down to us.

The crew of Miss Thangs sitting on the L-shaped couch may not have been too interested in Gee or Piper, but now they were eyeballing me and Raq, taking their time, checking us out, unabashedly trying to make sense of the new chicks on the scene. Despite their stares, most of them kept on nodding as if the same silent song were playing in all four of their heads, which I guess they thought was cute.

Finally, one of them spoke. She looked to be in her early twenties and had a horse's tail attached to the side of her head, but she at least scooted over to make room for us. "Here you go," she said without enthusiasm, gesturing to the spot she had cleared for us on the couch.

"Thanks." Raq played it cool and sweet as she sat down on the edge so that I could squeeze in between her and Ponytail

Girl. Her attitude as thick as the royal blue eyeliner she was wearing, the girl turned back to the television before continuing with her nodding. *Forget these two,* she and her friends seemed to be thinking. *It's all about us.*

"Yo . . ." Piper said, raising his hand in midair.

On cue, the girl on the far end of the couch tossed him a couch pillow. Piper tucked it behind his head and closed his eyes. Within moments his face relaxed and he was asleep. At first I thought, *He sure sleeps a lot,* but then I considered his schedule—how he's always traveling and performing somewhere and then has to go to the studio in the wee hours to record and it hit me—*No, he just sleeps when he can.*

With attitude, one of the girls demanded, "So where y'all from?"

Raq, playing it cool and nice, answered in a friendly voice. "Toledo."

Another girl said. "So y'all caught the show?"

"It was cool," Raq said. "Real cool."

Then Raq added, "I'm Raquel, by the way." She was so polite that it sounded like any second she would stand up and give a curtsy.

"Toya," Ponytail Girl offered, her big chandelier earrings moving as she spoke.

Following suit, they all introduced themselves like this was a routine that they were used to.

"Rishana," one said. She had big lips and gold shimmery lip gloss on top of them.

"Dee-Dee," the tiny light-skinned one with a messy, crinkled blonde weave down her back said.

"Kim," the thick one with braces said as she cracked her bubble gum.

And then they all just kept on nodding.

"I got some friends that live in Toledo," said Toya. "Heard they be having mad fun down there at the Quality."

"Oh, *the Q?*" Raq nodded and smiled convincingly. "That's our spot."

I kept a straight face but wished I could laugh. You had to be like twenty-five to get inside the Quality Bar.

"Y'alls zoo is kinda fly, too," offered Toya. "When we was kids, Granddaddy took us there once. Me and Gee."

Granddaddy? Gee had said his sister was having a Halloween party, so I guessed this meant Toya was his sister. I looked closer at her face. She and Gee were the same skin complexion, but that was about it. I never would have known they were related. He was so big and burly, and she was so small and wiry.

"Yeah," said Raq, who had—I knew for a fact—never been to the Toledo Zoo. "Our zoo is definitely tight."

Toya said, "My big-head brother hated it though. Complained the whole time about all the walkin'. He lazy."

The conversation went on like this—staggered fluff talk—for a while and eventually Raq and Toya seemed like easy buddies.

I just have my laws for power, Raq would explain to me the next day.

Be charming and kind when you're new on the scene.

Make calculated small talk.

Never—ever—try and trump the queen on your first move.

Raq would also explain that she could tell Toya was the queen because she had offered us a seat. She was the shot caller.

Tapping her toe to mine, Raq jerked her head a bit and bugged her eyes, a clear gesture for me to talk. Was she serious? The dead serious look in her eyes said yes, she was. I'd have much rather just sat back and watched. Raq was at ease with lying. I wasn't. I wasn't good at any of this.

But no. Sitting back and watching was what Ann Michelle would have done.

Glitz.

Glitz.

Glitz.

Just. Be. Glitz.

Despite my nervousness and the sweat in my palms, I unzipped my hoodie and felt around in my pocket for nothing. "Hey, I'm Glitz," I informed them. Then, to Toya, I said, "Cute ponytail."

"Glitz?" She grinned. "That's dope." Then she stroked her hair. "Yeah, I wasn't about to pay thirty dollars for a ponytail in a plastic bag when I could make it myself."

"I know that's right," Rishana co-signed. "These costume places kill me. Charging all that money . . ."

So they were wearing *costumes*? I had thought that was just the way they dressed.

Toya and the other girls turned back toward the TV and they all quickly became preoccupied with watching some old lady chase a dog down the street with a stick on *AFHV.* Raq joined them in laughing, but I did not. It was all still sinking in with me. I was here. This was really happening. I was sitting at a house party in Detroit. With Piper.

As if he could tell I was thinking about him, Piper stirred and cracked one eye open. "Yo . . . What's so hilarious?"

Dee-Dee, who had thrown Piper the pillow, said, "Pipe, take yourself on back to sleep."

"Yo . . . I'm not sleep . . . " he slurred.

In unison, all four girls finished his sentence: "Just relaxing my eyelids."

I studied what they were wearing, trying to guess who they were supposed to be dressed as. I didn't have a clue.

Dee-Dee caught me looking and chuckled. "What's wrong? You looking all confused. . . ."

Something about the way she was smiling and waiting made

me feel comfortable enough to be honest. "Just trying to figure out the costumes," I said.

Toya laughed, too. "Well, I'm *supposed* to be Sister Souljah. Bet if I woulda walked up in here looking like Lil' Kim, y'all woulda got it right."

Oh! Come to think of it, Sister Souljah *was* known for that ponytail on the side of her head. I looked back at Dee-Dee.

"Duh," she widened her eyes and laughed some more. "I'm Beyoncé!"

And sitting next to her, all fancy and glittery, I realized, was the rest of Destiny's Child. . . . Kelly and Michelle.

"Old-school." Dee-Dee smiled.

¤ ✖ ¤

The longer I sat, the heavier my eyes got. And then my back began aching from sitting still for so long.

I wondered what was keeping Sir Gee from coming back downstairs. I couldn't tell if Raq was speculating as well, because she was just leaned back watching *The Fresh Prince of Bel-Air*, which had come on after *America's Funniest Home Videos*; listening to Piper on the sound system; and looking breezy like everyone else.

Finally, the pool and dice games ended with sporadic curse words and the guys who had been playing came into the living room. From the questions like, "You ready, baby?" and "Where the keys, baby?" I could tell that they had come to gather their girlfriends. All but Toya got up to leave.

She clicked off the television and the stereo, then walked everyone to the back door. Moments later, the house much quieter now, I could hear her clogged heels clicking as she made it back up the hallway and reappeared in front of us. Other than that, there was only the sound of Piper snoring softly and me and Raq breathing.

Piper was asleep. Sir Gee was AWOL. And Toya was staring at us with a bored expression. *What now?*

She put her hand on her hip. "Up the steps, down the hall, last door on the right," she said. "That's the stray room."

"Excuse me?" Raq said with some attitude. Finally the real Raq was back. "Where's Greg? I don't know nothing about—"

"My brother is knocked out," Toya explained sans pretense or sass. "He real cool people and everything, don't get me wrong, but he's flat-out rude when he's tired. Straight up? He probably took a drink and hasn't thought twice about y'all since his feet hit them steps. In fact, tomorrow, you'll probably have to remind both of them who y'all are and how y'all even met."

I shot a look at Raq. Great. *Now how was I gonna get home?*

But Raq didn't bother to look at me. In fact, she didn't even flinch.

Then I thought about it. Raq wasn't the average chick. No

one could forget her. Maybe they wouldn't remember *me*, but Raq would be etched in their minds.

Toya said, "They do a show. Some random groupies latch on, hard pressed to hang with dudes they think about to be all the way large, and then they end up here. Then I gotta show 'em the stray room. And Pipe?" She shook her head before going over to the closet, grabbing a green blanket from the shelf, and—in one grand sweep—tossing warmth over Piper's body. She said, "My cousin has never known how to rest like a normal person. Sleeps in spurts."

Wow. Sir Gee and Piper were cousins? I hadn't read that one anywhere.

"Y'all from cross the line so, unless y'all got a car—which most of y'all strays don't—it's too late to be headed back to Ohio. So if y'all trying to stay, I don't mean to be ill, but I do call it the stray room for a reason."

Toya headed toward the steps and, realizing our limited options, we creaked up behind her. The upstairs hallway was unusually wide and everything smelled sock-drawer stuffy. We followed her past a couple of doors until we reached the last one on the right.

"You gone haveta excuse my brother," she said. "His manners are just whack sometimes, you know? But he's a dude, so . . . But hey, here you go . . ."

She pushed open the door to reveal two twin-sized beds with

nonmatching flowered comforters and a long metal dresser. It looked more like a small army barracks than a bedroom. But at least we could catch some Zs.

Toya stood there rubbing her eyes for a second. "I don't know nothing about either of you so I'll just let you know now, I'm a real light sleeper and I don't deal well with drama. Nursing school is kicking my ass, and I need all the rest I can get. Shoot. So let's just get some sleep, all right?"

"Thanks," I said.

"Oh," she continued, "don't bother trying to wake Gee. He hibernates like a big-assed bear and it's straight ridiculous if he wakes too soon. Piper, though? He gets up randomly. He never sits still for long, no matter how tired he is. I keep tellin' him all that stop-and-go stuff is gonna catch up with him, that he's gonna have a sleep disorder or somethin', but he's got his own mind, you know. Always had." She laughed. "I don't have no kids, but I got my brother and my cousin. . . . Crazy, right?" She yawned through a chuckle.

"Yeah," Raq added. "And thanks. For the room."

Toya said, "Oh, it's cool. But, um, basically, if you need something, bother Pipe, not me. Y'all set?"

Raq plopped down on one of the beds. "I think so."

"Thanks again, Toya," I added.

"Yuuuup," she replied, pulling the door closed behind her.

Raq waited until Toya's footsteps faded up the hallway. She shook her head. "You believe this? The *stray room*."

I shrugged. "And she seems so used to it. . . ."

A loud ticking sound demanded that we look at the clock on the dresser—5:59.

Whoa.

If Gramma only knew where I was.

As long as I was home first thing in the morning, she would never know. "Hey," I asked Raq, "You do think they're gonna take us home when we get up, right?"

Raq took a deep breath and fell back on one of the beds. "Would you *chill*? Of course," she said. "Quit worrying. In a few hours, you'll be home and your grandmother will be so over it, all right?"

I walked over to the dresser and set the clock for 7:30 A.M., which is when I'm usually on my way out the door on school days. Today, though, was Sunday. I just needed to make sure I had enough time to get home before Gramma got in from church. She would skin my behind if she knew I was about to lie down in some complete stranger's house, that in the morning while she was getting ready to play piano for the choir I would be trying to make it back to Toledo from Detroit after having been in the *hood* all night at that.

The beds looked lumpy but comfortable. I crawled onto the empty one, took off my hoodie, and rolled back the comforter.

The sheets were stiff and fresh pressed like a hotel room's and the pillow was too soft for my liking, but I wasn't about to complain. I just wanted to rest.

I could feel Raq staring at me and I could tell she was still sitting up in bed wanting to talk. I didn't look at her. Instead, I buried my head in the pillow and closed my eyes.

She said, "So what'd you think of Buckstarr?"

I waited a moment. Was she talking about her singing or her pushing up on Sir Gee? I couldn't tell. "She sounded all right," I said. "Not as good as you, though."

Raq sucked her teeth. "That skank."

I wanted to laugh. Too tired. "Hmmm . . ." came out instead.

Raq slapped a switch on the wall and the room slammed into darkness.

Moments later, her voice filled the room again. "I wish I didn't have to go back."

"Back where?" I replied.

"Dang, *chica*. You that sleepy?" She chuckled. "Where you think?"

"Oh." I fought my mind to stay awake longer, but I was so exhausted and I'm sure my voice was slurry. "So stay. You could live here in the stray room," I joked.

She was quiet and I got the feeling she was actually thinking about it. That was the difference between me and Raq. I knew when to stop fantasizing. She, on the other hand, did not. Sure, being with Piper and Gee had been amazing, but tomorrow we could just snap a picture and remember it always. At least we'd had tonight.

"*Don't*—I mean *dooooo not*—think for a second that I would do anything to jeopardize your education . . . or your precious little safety, *chica*," she said. "We'll make sure you're back in Gramma's house so you can be back in school on Monday morning to work on your—what—seven-point-nine grade point average? We wouldn't want her to worry aboutcha, now would we?"

"Whatever, Raq," I said, feeling a bit irritated by her suddenly sarcastic tone. "I'm just tired."

She cleared her throat. "Gee said he made a grand and a half tonight. And he's just a hype man, you know that? Following Piper around onstage, echoing his words. That's it. That's all he's gotta do. So imagine me on that hook, stacking paper just for doing my thing, *chica*! Can't you see it?"

"Of course, Raq," I said, thankful that it came out sounding convincing. Maybe now she would shut up and shut her eyes for a little while.

Finally, I heard her crawling under the covers.

But no. Still more.

"Gee said the crew is gonna be mad pissed. Well, really just Cyn 21. He said Cyn is all touched 'cause he didn't get in the booth tonight and he hasn't recorded in weeks. Cyn is really gonna flip when he finds out he's not even going on the road with him and Piper this week. . . ."

"Uh-huh," I said.

"You ever notice," Raq said, "every place I go, I'm a stray?"

She went on and on about how she had been a resident of countless juvenile detention centers, a foster child at so many houses she lost count after her twelfth placement, and always the new girl at school.

When it came to being a stray, she definitely had experience.

I was too tired to talk any more, though, so I faked a snore.

She whispered, "Dream about me, *chica.*"

Raq's voice lingered as I drifted off to sleep.

"Picture my name in the sky."

And so, as exhausted as I was, I imagined her name— Raquel Marissa Diaz—in glittered-out hot pink graffiti, the "i" dotted with a star, right up there shining.

10

"It's like that?"

The sound of someone shouting jerked me out of my sleep and for a moment I had to consciously try to remember where I was. The walls, more dingy in daylight, were startling and unfamiliar and so were the shouting voices. The digital clock read 8:28. There was the faint sound of the radio playing, a station not completely tuned in, and I realized that I'd slept right through the alarm.

I heard the door creaking open and then I saw Raq tiptoeing back into the room. I sat up in bed and stared out in the hallway. What was all the commotion about? And where was Raq coming from? I looked over at her bed. It appeared to have barely been slept in.

Another voice was shouting now. "You heard me! That's right . . . That's right . . ."

I looked at Raq. "What's going on?"

She shrugged. "Cyn is here. Him and Gee are going at it."

I crawled from underneath the covers and we tiptoed out of the room.

From the top of the stairs, we watched their heads. Sir Gee. Toya. Piper. And an aggravated Cyn 21 pacing back and forth, his face tight and fuming.

Toya's ponytail was replaced by a tight-fitting and brightly multicolored silk scarf. Standing in her fluffy house robe, she was snaking her neck back and forth, chandelier earrings she hadn't bothered to take off from last night now knocking her upside the head as she did. "Y'all *all* need to chill the hell out!" she shouted. "Take this mess outside! Fight in my house, I bet you I'm about to be done with all three of y'all."

"Yo . . ." Piper reached out for her hand. "No disrespect, Toya."

Toya snatched her hand away. "Too late," she said. "I'm tired of dealing with this again!"

Piper turned his attention back to Cyn 21. "Man, it don't even gotta be like this. You upset at the wrong people. This is me. Pipe."

"Sheeit . . ." Cyn 21 grunted. "Y'all *all* be on some real grimy stuff, I swear man. Y'all—"

"Y'all?" Piper's hand went to his chest and his knees bucked. "Cyn! Are you serious? Me? Piper?"

Cyn 21 didn't answer, but shot dagger eyes at Sir Gee.

Gee, dressed now in sweat clothes and a do-rag, threw

his hands in the air. "Oh, so I guess now *I'm* shady, huh? Now you think *I'm* trying to play you? Okay, first it's Piper . . ." Gee chuckled at the thought. "Piper's tryna play you. But now it's me, too? This paranoia is gettin' outta hand, Cyn."

"Yo . . ." Piper shook his head.

Toya was mumbling. "Take it outside . . . Take it outside . . ."

"Yo . . ." Piper pleaded, holding his hands as if he were praying, "Cyn, man, this is *us*. Me and Gee. Us three. We go back like eight tracks!"

Cyn smirked. "This really ain't got nothing to do with none of that, Pipe. That was some stupid stuff from back in the day. This here is for real. We grown."

Gee offered. "Well, you need to take it up with Mun. Me and Pipe didn't have nothing—"

Cyn eyed Gee. "Okay. So *Mun* told you to cut me out?"

Sir Gee groaned, "Man, I swear if you quote me on that, I'll—"

"Gee!" Cyn 21's chest swelled up and he stood, man-to-man, chest-to-chest, in front of Gee. "I'm *not* scared of Mun."

I inhaled. So did Raq. Together, we kept listening.

"Or you!" Cyn spat through his teeth. "Man, I stepped to you after the show, you like, '*Later, man* . . .' Then I try and holla at you up at the Waffle House, you like '*Later, man* . . .' Mun's buggin' in the studio, you like, '*Tomorrow, man* . . .' I'm up all night, no missed calls from you. So tell me"—Cyn glared—"how in the hell can *we* all play our positions when only you and Pipe on the field?"

Piper shook his head. "Cyn, man . . ."

Cyn 21 looked over at Piper and backed away from Gee. "Pipe, I got a son to feed. You know this."

Sir Gee fumed. "What? You think I'm tryna stop you from feeding your seed? It's like *that*?" He huffed. "And you got one more time to step up to my face again—"

Cyn immediately stepped to Sir Gee, tip of the nose to tip of the nose, nostrils flaring, "I call it like I see it, *punk.*"

Raq shot me a look and both of us held our breath.

Sir Gee glared at Cyn 21and Gee glared right back at him. Toya stood with her hand on the wall and head lowered, pleading for them to stop. It sounded like she was crying. Piper stood with his hands clasped and his eyes closed. Clearly, he was praying. And then . . .

"Yo . . ." Piper eased toward them. "Cyn"—he touched his shoulder.

Cyn jerked away and was staring Piper down now. He may have been much skinnier than Gee, but at least they were closer in height. Cyn was looking down at Piper.

"Yo . . . " Piper said, unaffected by Cyn's deadened eyes. "We gon' let this divide us, man? Some damn money? Paper? Man, you know I'm puttin' everybody on once I get on. I stack this paper this week, my word, you can have every dime."

Cyn cocked his neck. "Oh so now you tryna play me? Like *I'm* the only sucka lookin' to stack ends. What, you better than me? All you care about is music now? Since when?"

"Yo . . ." Piper shook his head. "All I'm sayin' is that we all gotta eat. But if this is what it is—money—then all I'm sayin'—"

"I *know*"—Gee, who had been locked into a frozen position, stepped closer to Cyn now—"you did not just come to my home with this bull."

Now Cyn and Gee were back in an eye war.

Toya shouted, "I-said-take-this-mess-*out*-of-my-house!"

That's when Cyn 21 reached into his pocket and grabbed hold of something.

Gee didn't budge. "Oh, so now you wanna shoot me? Who's the punk now?"

"Yo." Piper reached for the doorknob. "Cyn, you heard Toya, man. You can't be going there up in the crib like this."

"Y'all ain't even worth it, man." Cyn offered Gee one final face growl.

Piper grabbed Cyn's arm just as he went to leave, his voice pained but calm, "Yo—"

"Back off me, Pipe. Don't put your name on this bullet, either."

Piper let go. Took a step back. Hands up.

Cyn 21 shook his head, went to say something, changed his mind, then just shook his head again.

Sir Gee, however, was glaring as Cyn pulled open the door to leave. He said, "Cyn, you ever step to me again—ever in *life*—man, I swear you better—"

Just as the door slammed, Toya shouted, "Gee! He's gone. Just drop it!"

"Yo . . ." Piper tapped his forehead a few times in aggravation. "Gee, we're talking *dirt*, man. *Dirt.* That's what we're coming to? My homie? Talking bullets. Over paper? Paper from trees? Trees that grow from the ground? The ground, which is nothing but dirt?" He scrunched up his nose like he'd just smelled something disgusting. "Stankin' . . . Meaningless . . . Expendable . . . *Dirt*?" He waited. No response.

With the silence lingering, Raq and I tiptoed to the bathroom.

We fixed ourselves up on autopilot and I felt numb, shivering even though I wasn't cold. That argument had made Gramma's daily ranting seem like nursery rhymes.

Raq pressed her back to the door and looked serious, too. She put her fingers to her temples and rubbed. "That was nuts."

I nodded. And my heart was heavy. I just wanted to get home. Bullets meant guns. And guns meant bad, bad things. I'd had enough. More than enough.

Raq said, "Can you believe it? Just that quick, Cyn coulda snapped."

I took a towel from the wicker stand above the toilet and used liquid hand soap to wash my face. "I agree," I said, and then rumbled around in the cabinet for some mouthwash. I found Listerine and began to gargle.

"Where were you this morning?" I asked.

"Oh," she said, "I was talking to Gee."

"Really?"

"Yeah. Right before Cyn knocked on the door Gee said we should come with him and Piper on the road."

I looked at her to make sure I'd heard correctly. "Huh?"

Raq got a towel, too. She smiled and then matter-of-factly shrugged. "I say let's go."

I took a good spit. "Go *where*?"

"Gee says they're loading about five thousand CDs for the road. They don't have to be in New York until Thursday but they're doing general promo for Piper along the way. He said that's mostly what they do all the time, go out on the road, stop through parties and places and push CDs and stop through radio spots. When I told him we were trying to get to New York, too, he said we could roll as long as we help them give away some of Piper's promo CDs along the way."

"You told him *who* is trying to get to New York?"

"Us."

"Why would you tell him that?"

She laughed. "Because we are. Aren't we? The birthplace of hip-hop. It's our dream—"

"Yeah! *Someday.* Not now. Not when we're in high school! Maybe when we're older and grown and . . ."

"Why *not* now?" Her reflection watched mine in the mirror. "We have nothing to lose. And everything to gain."

I snickered. "Maybe *you* have nothing to lose—"

"Look. We'll be back in a week. And by then we'll be famous—"

"I never said I wanted to be a star."

"Okay, well then *I'll* be famous. And as my best friend, you'll meet famous people with me."

"Raq! I can't—"

"Greg said Piper's doing an appearance in Philly on Wednesday. Then he's got a big show in New York, that all-star tribute to Jam-Master Jay. *Chica* . . . Everybody who's ever been anybody or is gonna *be* somebody will be there. *And* it's at the Apollo. You know, *chica.* The Apollo? Come. On. There's no way I wouldn't leave the Apollo without meeting someone who could sign me to a label or produce my music or *something.* You know me!"

"Of course. But you *know* I have to go home."

She said, "They're leaving today. In a little bit . . ."

"Well as long as they stop through Toledo on the way, then they can drop me off."

Raq put her hand on my shoulder and forced me to look at her. "Okay, *mira* . . . Didn't I get us to meet Piper? Well, we'll meet Millionaire Mal, too, all right? And Fat Joe. And Pitbull. And I don't even know who else. Whoever else you wanna meet—"

"Raquel!" I jerked away from her. "Are you crazy? I can't go to New York. Wake up from this dream, okay? My grandmother would murder me with one smack!"

"Chica." She put her hand right back on my shoulder. "You'll be back in less than a week! The show is Thursday night and I'll flap my arms and fly you home myself on Saturday if I have to. I promise. First class if you want, even! All we gotta do is make it to that show at the Apollo. *Chica!* It's the friggin' Jam-Master Jay tribute! You think I wouldn't be all up around all those heavyweights coming in to pay homage to Jay and I'm not gonna come out with a record deal?"

Gramma would kill me.

Plus, things were scary now. It was one thing to listen to songs about guns. But now I'd practically seen one. I wanted to be right there with Raq for every part of her rise to fame, but not yet. After high school and once we had enough money saved up to do it right.

With pleading eyes, she said. "Come on! Don't you wanna be there too? With me? You're my best friend. *Mi hermana . . ."*

I looked at her. And she at me.

Real face to real face now.

"Please," she said. "I've never had a friend like you, *chica.*

I know I can make it, I know I can, but with you there with me, like, there's no doubt in my mind. It's the chance of a lifetime and I've never in my life had anyone riding with me the way you do. Not even my own mother. I'm gonna be famous, *chica*, and I need you with me. I can't do this without you." It sounded a little like Raq was going to cry. I'd never seen her show a soft side like this before.

"But my grand—"

"Your Gramma will be fine! Even *she* is going to laugh about it someday, too, all right?" She laughed playfully but her eyes looked a little wet. "We'll buy her a fancy dress for the Grammy party. She'll toast to us and say, 'Oh I remember that time when my granddaughter was gone for a week and had me all worried. And now look at her. Rich. Mixing with the stars . . .'"

No way would Gramma *ever* find any of this funny, trust me. Not even two thousand years from now. Please. Jay Leno was pretty much the only thing that I'd ever seen that could make her laugh. *Ever.*

Raq really was my best friend, though. My only friend, in fact. And I really did believe in her.

I said, "And say *what* to my grandmother in the meantime, Raq? She'll be stressed sick. She'll—"

"You'll be *back* in a week," Raq grabbed both of my shoulders now. "I *promise*. Haven't I done everything I said I would do? I had your back when the Prissycat Dolls dissed you, right? I quit my job so we could make it to the concert. I got us *in*. And didn't I get us backstage? *I'll get you back home!* You have to—''

BOOM.

And then a scream from downstairs.

The blast made both of us jump.

Toya's shrill shriek was deafening. Her scream filled the entire house. Every muscle in my body turned to wet bread, heavy and mushy.

''Oh God.'' Raq grabbed her chest. ''Oh God.''

She yanked open the door, grabbed my hand, and pulled me along as we ran down the stairs.

Both of us froze at the last step, staring straight ahead at the front door to the house.

Sir Gee was standing by the open door, looking out onto the porch, and his expression was solemn. His face flinched a bit, but he didn't say a word. He just stood there with his jaws clenched and his eyes narrow.

Toya was standing there, too, and I saw her fist slam against the wall. I watched as she snatched a plastic pumpkin from last night and vomited into it.

Piper. Only he had the nerve to step out on the porch. Cyn 21's crisp damaged jeans and black Timberlands were all I could make out from where I stood. He was lying there on the ground.

I was too scared to move closer. I could see Piper's back as he leaned down over Cyn's body. His head dropped as he called back over his shoulder to Gee. "Yo . . . He ain't dead, man. He's just . . ." And then his voice cracked.

Gee whipped out his cell phone and called 911.

"I need an ambulance . . . My homie . . . Just put a gun on himself . . . On my porch . . . No ma'am . . . Yes ma'am . . . Antuan Cyndell Carter . . ."

After Gee hung up from the call, he pulled Toya to his chest, muffling her cries. Neither of them looked out onto the porch where Piper stayed crouched beside Cyn murmuring encouragement.

"Yo . . . you gonna be all right, man. You hear me? Keep looking at me, man. . . ."

My eyes felt too heavy as the hot tears flowed.

I could hear Cyn moaning and then Piper hushing him.

"Don't try to talk, man . . ."

I'd never really paid much attention to Cyn 21's career, couldn't quote any of his bars if I tried, but I knew that he'd always seemed angry in his rhymes, and in person, too. And I knew from this morning that he had big dreams just like the rest of them. Desperate dreams.

Sir Gee put in another call while we waited. "S'up, Mun?" He said. "It's wild . . ."

Raq went over to console Toya, who was still weeping, while Gee explained things to Mun.

I sat next to Toya on the couch as Raq held her from the other side. Toya's crying was causing the whole couch to shake. And I listened as Gee put in yet another phone call. From what he said, I figured he was talking to Cyn's girlfriend.

"Hey Dana, babygirl . . . Bad news, babygirl . . . Naw . . . Yeah . . . Not sure. But he needs you. You got somebody to watch Lil' Man? Naw. You better not. . . . Okay . . . The ambulance is on the way. . . ."

I couldn't move for so long.

Silence. But so much noise.

Sirens.

Voices.

Clanking. Grunting. More clanking.

Doors opening. Doors slamming.

More voices. A scream.

Clanking. Clanking. Clanking.

Doors opening. Doors slamming.

The sirens again.

Piper's eyes were swollen red when he finally came back inside, after the EMTs took Cyn away. His voice cracked and he didn't look at any of us directly when he spoke.

He said, "He didn't do what he tried to do. But yo . . . He definitely tried."

Toya was rocking back and forth.

Gee was slamming CDs into a box.

For a while, Piper stood staring out the window. But soon, he gave Gee a hand.

Toya said, "I got love for all y'all. I swear. But this music stuff ain't worth it, if it's gotta come to this. People goin' crazy . . ."

Gee stopped then and looked at her dead-on. "*Don't* start with that, Toya."

Piper offered a sympathetic raised eyebrow to her. "You all right?"

She wiped her face and smacked her lips. "What you mean am I all right? Are *you* all right? Y'all just packing up for the road, acting like it's nothing."

A part of me felt like we should go back upstairs and give them their privacy, but things were happening so fast. What if we did and they all left and forgot about us? How would I get home?

"Yo—" Piper said.

"Toya!" Gee interrupted before Piper could respond. "You need to calm down with all that. You know damn well that man got issues deep. Not a damn thing any of us can do to fix the demons in that man's mind. Be happy he can get some help now."

But Toya just kept on rocking back and forth, looking both sad and aggravated, not bothering to comment.

Now Piper looked at Raq. And then me. "Y'all all right?"

"Yeah." Raq's voice was quiet.

I asked, "So is he going to be okay?"

Piper reached into his pocket and retrieved a small copper bullet. He kissed it and put it back. "Just grazed him. But yo . . . he's gonna have a helluva headache." He said, "Yo . . . All respect to Cyn, Toya, but—"

"But nothin', Pipe," Toya said. "Just go on. Y'all just go on and do what y'all do best. Hit the road and do music. *I'll* be here for Dana and A. J. How's that?"

Gee groaned, then grabbed a bag and a box of CDs and took them into the kitchen. I heard the back door slam and figured he must have gone out to start loading up the car.

Piper, though, kissed Toya on the cheek, her eyes falling closed when he did.

"Yo . . ." Piper said. "If I thought I could fix Cyn, Toya, you know I'd be the first man to do it. But we all know Piper don't have the recipe for that potion. You say 'go do what we do' like it's a crime or somethin', like it's a bad thing. We all gotta give a gift to the world. Yours is taking care of folks. I'll pray for Cyn, but mine is somethin' else, all right? And I gotta do it."

Toya appeared to ease up a little. "Y'all be careful," she said.

Piper looked at me and Raq. "Train is ready to choo-choo. Anybody rollin' . . . Let's."

Raq got up first. Of *course* she was down.

Only I still wasn't sure. Sure, I *wanted* to go. But . . .

Piper noticed me sitting.

"Yo . . ." he said. "Ready, Glitz?"

A stray.

And yet he remembered my name.

How would I find the strength, the heart, the right moment, to remind him to drop me off at home?

11

I-75 again.

Going south.

Right past Toledo.

We were riding in Gee's black Hummer. Gee and Piper were up front and Raq sat in the back with me, much easier for her to keep giving me those pleading eyes. Her best friend, how could I *not* go with her? Gramma raised me because my parents couldn't do so from heaven, because *I* needed *her*. But this was different. Now someone needed *me*.

Raq convinced Piper and Gee to stop at Target so we could pick up a few things for the road. Once inside, Raq whisked up the aisles, throwing this and that into the cart I was pushing. We both needed jeans and a few cute tops, I remember her saying. She also bought us all the basic toiletries and swiped the debit card her foster parents had given her when we checked out. I tried to pitch in with what little cash I had, but Raq said not to worry about it.

"You're coming along on this trip for me, *chica*," she said as she flipped through a magazine at the check-out, then tossed it on the register belt as well. "Buying you a few things is the least I can do."

"I'll pay you back," I assured her. I felt bad that I didn't have the money to buy my own stuff, but Gramma didn't believe in kids having credit cards *or* debit cards—she just gave me my allowance in cash every week. And I had left the house last night with only twenty dollars in my wallet. I had never imagined needing more.

Raq rolled her eyes playfully. "I won't need it after this week, *chica*. Trust me."

After shopping we returned to the Hummer, me and Raq still behind Sir Gee and Piper, both of whose seats were pushed all the way back. Even still, Raq and I had plenty of room. The truck was just that big. Everyone was talking, but it all sounded like a blur to me. I may have added to the conversation or maybe I just sat there, I can't remember. I was in a stupor, in awe of my own nerve. I was officially on the road with Piper MC and my best friend. Raq was right. Gramma would just *have* to get over it. What could she do, really? Disown me? Lock me away for ten years? Whatever punishment she chose, this week had better be worth it. Already, Piper knew my name. And I was on my way to New York.

I glanced up ahead at the clock—2:49.

Gramma was probably home from church by now, calling out to the Lord and the police, too. I had never done anything this crazy, and I'm sure she never imagined I would. Eventually I would have to call her, I knew, but what would I say?

As we merged onto I-280, toward Cleveland's portions toll that would take us farther east, I closed my eyes and breathed deeply. With Toledo now literally behind us, Raq tapped my arm a few times, squirming with joy. I was officially gone. Might as well enjoy it.

Miles later, as we merged onto I-80 for the straightaway toward Cleveland, an autumn storm began stirring in the charcoal gray sky. November first. The rain swayed the truck a bit, but no one suggested pulling over until the weather cleared. Determined. Each of us were. Gee wanted to make it. And to make sure Piper did. Raq wanted to make it. And to make sure I was with her. Piper wanted to make music. And he wanted people to love it.

Glitz was going to just try to be happy for getting to be a part of it all.

As for Ann Michelle? Who cared what she wanted.

I stared out the window, rain beating against the glass like pennies falling from the sky. I put a smile on my face and leaned back against my seat, listening to Piper's music. Nothing was going to stop us.

A few hours into the drive, we pulled over at an Ohio turnpike rest stop, one of those domed buildings that house a few fast food restaurants and maybe a souvenir shop or two. I don't even remember anyone saying they were hungry. It was unspoken. Or maybe Gee and Piper just needed some air. So much had happened today.

We slammed our doors and splashed through the water as we ran to get inside. The rest stop was full with laughter and conversation—families on road trips, businesspeople on cell phones, truck drivers joking or looking tired. I saw a security guard in the doorway, eating a hot dog, and hoped he wouldn't look our way when we walked in. What if Gramma had called the police?

Raq looked over at me.

I looked back at her.

She widened her eyes.

I pleaded back with mine. *What*?

She mouthed the word "Relax . . ."

I was doing my best.

Sir Gee asked Piper what he wanted and Piper told him: two chicken sandwiches and a strawberry shake. "I got you, *chica*," Raq said, tapping her pocket. Knowing my usual, a Whopper Jr. with cheese and fries and a chocolate shake—she joined Sir Gee at the counter to purchase our food while Piper and I searched for a clean table.

He sat down across from me and started talking. "Yo . . . Out here in the rap game, a man just wants to get in, you know? With anything though, a rapper, a hoop star, a tycoon, whatever, at the end of the day we're all just brothas wanting to do their thing, ya dig? We all just want to get closer to the stake than the next man. Figure if we can just get close enough, closer than the next man . . . Me and Cyn? Not really that different, you know?"

Piper squinted his eyes and then closed them. Sitting across from me in that booth, at some random rest stop in Ohio, Piper wasn't the man who had played to a sold-out show at the old VFW in Toledo last night. All of a sudden he was a small-framed, chestnut-skinned, dreadlock-wearing, tattooed-out twenty-something-year-old trying to make sense of what had happened to his friend.

I said. "How long have you known him?"

"Ol' Cyn?" He kinda smiled. "Yo . . . He never wanted much, you know? See, comin' up out our hood into this here game . . . It's like we're walking on ice, but it's like it's nothing but fire underneath us, trying to melt away our chance to keep going . . . Underneath us is just fire . . . threatening our dreams. . . ."

He paused for a moment.

"I've known him for a long time," he said. Then he smiled at me. "My whole life . . ." He gazed off into the distance. Eerie.

Quiet. Frozen. And then, "Just the chance to make music. That's all he ever wanted. . . . Any of us."

"Piper, I'm real sorry about your friend . . . But I'm real glad it looked like he's gonna be okay. You think?"

He looked at me and smiled. "Yo . . ." he said. "I appreciate that. He will. He's gotta be, you know?"

In that moment, I knew it was worth it. All the trouble I was sure to be in with Gramma. To be sitting here in Akron, Ohio, making Piper smile.

"Ay," Sir Gee's voice snapped me to attention as he and Raq approached the table with trays full of food. "We about to get sick wit' all this food," he said, ready to inhale all that he'd purchased. Piper said grace—"Yo, thank you, Lord for this food. Bless the hands that prepared it. Bless us as we consume it. Bless those who don't have it"—and then, we slammed.

Piper started it first, making silly toasts with our milkshakes.

"Yo . . . here's to fine dining at Burger King."

Raq laughed real loud and posted up her shake as well. "And to fly riding in a Hummer . . ."

Sir Gee laughed, "To Nuuuu Yorrrrk. Here we come, big pimpin'."

We cracked up.

"Yo . . ." Piper said. "To Big Pun . . ."

Raq said, "To Pac . . ."

Sir Gee added, "Jam-Master . . ."

Piper said, "To Cyn . . ."

A hush. Then we all smiled and toasted again.

Piper added, "To better days for him . . ."

"For all of us," Gee added. Then we toasted some more.

"To hip-hop," Piper said.

I said, "And to Piper MC."

Everyone raised the milkshakes just a tad higher this time and chimed in, "To Piper."

Piper said, "Yo . . . I can't wait for New York."

"You ain't never lied," Gee offered. "I can smell them funky-assed streets already."

We all laughed.

"So um . . ." Raq said, "is Buckstarr coming, too?"

Sir Gee let out a loud guffaw. "Naw! She gotta tape some reunion for her show—what is it Pipe?"

"Flavor of Chance When I Wanna Be a Housewife or a Bachelorette and Dance with an Idol."

"Yeah." Gee stuffed a bunch of french fries in his mouth and chuckled. "That show."

We all laughed.

Raq grinned. "Bummer. I thought she seemed real cool at the studio. Woulda been cool to hang with her."

Raq nodded. "And I was hoping I would get to see her perform live Thursday, you know? She's real good on 'Liar, Liar.' That's my jam . . ."

And finally, Raq saw the opportunity to give Sir Gee and Piper what she'd been holding inside. In a voice raspy like Mariah's but soulful like Mary J's and in a register sincere like a blues singer, she surprised even me.

> *Ooooohhhh . . .*
> *Liar . . .*
> *A liar I desire . . .*
> *Set my heart on fire . . .*
> *I lovvvve you . . .*
> *Oh yeah.*

Raq had the melody down but her tone was different from Buckstarr's. More sorrowful. More sincere. Less sexy than Buckstarr's and more aching. It was more hip-hop meets the blues, less sex kitten. Judging from the silence around us and Sir Gee's and Piper's eyes on Raq, I knew I wasn't the only one affected.

"Yo . . ." A smile crept onto Piper's face, his interest piqued. "What's your full name again?"

She smiled. "Raquel Marissa Diaz. But Raq is cool."

Never try and trump the queen on your first move.

Wait. And be calculated.

12

Me and my best friend. *Check.*

The hottest up-and-coming hip-hop star. *Check.*

On our way to New York City, the birthplace of hip-hop. *Check.*

Freedom from the drudgery of school and my grandmother. *Check. Check.*

No rules. No limitations. Just excitement, hope, and possibility.

It was a fantasy come true and I wanted to believe in it.

Instead, all I kept thinking about was Gramma.

Gramma.

Gramma.

Gramma.

Later, we stopped at another rest stop, and me and Raq went to use the restroom. It was the evening by that point, and according to Gee, we were less than forty miles away from Pittsburgh. I could hear her cell phone vibrating incessantly, and as soon as it would stop, it would begin again, adamant and obnoxious. I had heard it doing that all day but had tried to convince myself the calls were for Raq, not for me.

I was standing at the rust-stained metal sink, brushing my hair into a fresh ponytail, when Raq slipped her phone from under the stall she was in. I peered down at the stark bright screen, now tinted blue, and it was screaming A. MICHELLE'S GRANNY like a broken traffic light. *Bizzzzzzzz. Bzzzz. Bzzzzzzzzzzzzzzzzzzzzzz.*

Finally, I snatched the phone from Raq and pressed SEND to answer it. "Hello?"

I heard Raq gasp and then giggle. I held my breath, having no idea what I was going to say next.

Gramma sounded relieved. "Oh, Ann! Is that you?" she said.

An impossible weight of guilt fell into my stomach. "Hi, Gramma . . ."

She cheered. "Where are you?"

I leaned against the bathroom wall. The tile felt so cold. This whole morning of being free and on the road had felt like a foggy fantasy. Now it was time to come back to a clear reality. "I'm at Raq's," I said, wondering how I was going to say the same thing tomorrow, too, and then again the next day.

With the relieved smile fading from her voice, Gramma replied, "Well, I'll just come on and pick you up. Since apparently you missed *first thing in the morning* this morning. You got homework I need to check?"

I banged my head against the wall. My eyes fixed on the ceiling, I said, "Gramma, it's okay. Raq just ordered a pizza. We're gonna eat and then—"

"And when you get home," she said, her voice forcefully calm, "I'm taking you in for a drug screen. Just say yes or no . . . Has that child exposed you to smoking things?"

"*Right!* Gramma, come on. I'm sixteen years old. Why do you talk to me like I'm a kid?"

She sounded cross now. "Child, I know how old you are!" And then: "Are y'all somewhere having sex with boys?"

"Gramma! You're *not* serious!" Gramma has Raq pinned as some weed-smoking promiscuous girl, but in one of our first serious conversations, Raq had confided in me that she was still a virgin, and that she hated drugs because of what they'd done to her mother.

Gramma continued, "I'm coming to get you. Right now. Put your shoes and socks on. What's the address?"

I took a purposefully long deep breath. "I'm just . . . I need to . . ."

"You need to *what*?" Gramma asked in her no-nonsense voice.

I swallowed. "I'm uh . . ."

It was official—God had completely tied my tongue and deserted me. I couldn't even *think* of a lie.

Without my permission, panic slipped out with my words and my voice cracked. I said, "I'm sorry. Okay? Gramma, I..."

She sounded as angry as she did confused. "Sorry? For what—"

I pulled the phone from my ear, put my hand to my chest, and felt my heartbeats.

Standing in front of me now, Raq pulled the phone from my hand and pressed END. Just like that, she'd dismissed it all.

"Anyhow. Did you see how they looked at me, *chica*? They know I'm better than Buckstarr for that hook. She ain't got nothing on your girl!" She tousled her hair a bit. "That song is *mine* by the time we get to New York."

Raq clearly didn't want to talk about what had just happened with Gramma, and I didn't want to either. I was disappointing my grandmother, something I had never done before, and I felt horrible. But on the other hand, I felt a little free. This was my life, wasn't it? And this was my time to live it. Going on the road with Piper was a one-in-a-million opportunity, something Gramma wasn't going to understand.

I tried to smile in agreement as I brushed my ponytail some more.

"By the way," Raq said. "The whole ponytail thing is gettin' played, all right?"

I looked in the mirror, turned my head, and checked my side profile. Raq was right. But without a flat iron, curling iron, or anything else, what else could I do?

Raq reached up and slid the rubber band from my hair. She finger combed it down until it hung straight. Despite the dent from the elastic, it actually looked okay.

"I'll do some spirals or something when we can get us a curling iron. And stop looking so worried," she warned me. And then she smiled. "We *belong* here, *chica*! This is our world. We gotta act like we own this. Your grandmother will be fine. She heard your voice and now she's got no reason to worry. She knows you're not dead. Now she'll just be mad. And since she's already mad, you might as well enjoy this. You're here now. Don't let her ruin it for you."

Raq was right, I knew, but there was a part of me that wasn't so sure that Gramma wouldn't take some extreme measure. *Wonder if she's calling the police right this second.* At the very least I figured she'd call Raq's foster parents. I had told her their names when I first started hanging out with Raq. I thought knowing that Raq had had a hard life would make Gramma go a little easier on her. I was so wrong.

On the way back to the car, Raq suggested that we stop in the gift shop and get some stuff. We grabbed a red plastic basket and tossed in candy and chips, sodas and gum, T-shirts and yo-yos, magazines and coloring books, a Slinky and Silly Putty. As usual, Raq didn't bother to look at any of the price tags. I wondered how much money she even had on her debit card. Must've been plenty.

I noticed a shelf full of Ohio postcards and maps on a turnstile by the counter. Without meaning to, I started to reminisce. When I was little, Gramma and I traveled this very turnpike heading to Cedar Point in Sandusky, the best amusement park in the world. Sometimes we passed by here to go to Hershey, Pennsylvania, too. We used these very roads to get to Pittsburgh, where we'd visit my great-aunt Maybel, Gramma's older, meaner, and even more religious sister. While she and Gramma had Bible study with church ladies, they'd enroll me in some church camp where all the kids would want to play and laugh and be silly together but mostly we had to learn Bible verses and be serious. There was one teacher—Sister Jo—who was nice, though. She'd let us go outside at the end of the day if we were well behaved and sometimes she'd even join us in puff-blowing on dandelions. Honestly, I never minded the lessons on God and the verses we had to memorize. The hymns really were lovely to me. But all I ever wanted was just to have a little fun, too, to feel free.

Raq emptied the basket and plunked everything down on the counter.

The owl-faced lady rang up our goods. "Sixteen twenty-three," she announced, and Raq handed over her card. This time I caught a glimpse of it: American Express. Wow. Must be nice. I thought she just had a debit card. I didn't know Raq was balling like that. I didn't know a whole lot about credit cards, but I thought that was a fancy one.

At the last second, I reached back over and grabbed a postcard and slid the cashier the fifty cents for it. I thought maybe I'd send it to Gramma. I was showing Raq the card and we were whispering about how crazy it was going to be when Gramma got it in the mail when our talking was interrupted by a loud beep.

"Your card's been declined," the cashier said. "And there's a message to call the credit card company." And just that quick, the lady was dialing.

I was going to offer to pay with cash—I still had that same twenty dollars I took with me last night—but then I realized I should hold on to it in case I really needed something later on. I felt bad, though. Raq had already spent so much on me.

"Oh, that's okay," Raq said. "We'll just pass on all this stuff." She reached over at the register and tried to take back her card, cool and smiling, like it was no big deal. I didn't think it was a big deal either. Gramma's card had been declined once because she grabbed one that had expired a long time ago—

she had forgotten to cut it up—and the cashier gave it back to her without event.

But *this* lady snatched the card back from Raq's reach and kept the phone to her ear.

"Chica," Raq said under her breath, turning to leave, "let's go . . ."

Right on her heels, I followed.

Once we got to the door, Raq said, *"Runnnn!"*

And we did.

I had no idea why.

And my heart was skyrocketing.

We piled into the backseat of the truck and Gee turned back to look at us. "What y'all doing? Racing or something?"

"Yeah," Raq said, out of breath. "We can't wait to get to New York."

I tried holding my breath to calm my heart, but it was beating so loud I was sure Gee and Piper could hear it.

"Yo . . ." Piper said. "Y'all all out of breath and thangs." He laughed.

Gee pulled off and rolled through the parking lot without asking any questions, but I was sitting behind him and I peeped the look in his eyes in the rearview mirror. He was looking back at me, so I offered a smile, hoping he would think that everything was okay. Finally, he shifted his eyes away and concentrated on the road. I wished I could do the same.

The car was silent for the next few miles, but eventually we all started talking again. Like it had never even happened. But it had. It definitely had.

⋈

WELCOME TO PENNSYLVANIA, the sign read.

It felt like we'd been on the road forever when we finally left Ohio and headed into Pennsylvania toward Pittsburgh. The simple landscape gave way to winding roads and majestic hills and grand mountainsides. There was a difference, too, in Gee's driving. Slower. Less persistent. Until finally he asked, "Wanna just get a room?"

Sounding exhausted, Piper replied. "Might as well."

I looked at the clock. It was only 9:32. But so much had happened that day that I guess all of us needed to rest.

I was approaching twenty-four hours past curfew now.

I hoped we were getting two separate rooms. Piper and Gee were cool, but I wasn't comfortable sleeping in the same room with them. And I couldn't *wait* to shower.

Plus, me and Raq needed to talk.

"How the heck are we going to pay for a room, Raq?" I whispered to Raq. "That lady took your card, didn't she? I only have twenty dollars. . . ."

With an annoyed expression on her face, she pulled a

National City Bank debit card from her purse. Her name, she made sure I could see, was written across the front.

⌗ ▨ ⌗

On the double bed next to mine, in a room adjacent to Piper and Sir Gee's, at a random Holiday Inn Express, Raq lay on her stomach on a flower-print bedspread still hinting of cigarettes from the guest before us. She closed her eyes and pressed her face to a pillow she'd just balled up. Directly across from her on the other bed, I sat erect and nervous. We were miles away from the rest-stop incident, but it was still very much on my mind. She, on the other hand, seemed totally at ease.

"How are we going to pay for the rest of this week—food, motels, all that stuff?" I asked.

"I've got at least four hundred cash." Raq turned her head slightly and let her big brown eyes drift open again so she could get a good look at me. "Okay?"

Wow. Four hundred bucks? Jeez. Maybe Kitty's brother could hook *me* up with the job Raq had just quit.

Then she said, "I was saving it for the mall, but we can use some for the motel, too. I was thinking . . . We really need to get to a store where we can take our time and find us some *really* fly gear for New York."

"Okay, but what was all that about at the rest stop? Why didn't you wait to get your card back?"

She grunted. "Oh my goodness, *chica*! Loosen *up*. That lady is probably waiting on some old man buying Depends by now. You think she's worried about *us*? Come on." With a crooked little smile she said, "Besides, catching Raquel Marissa Diaz has *never* been done. Okay?"

"Excuse me?" I said. "Catching you . . . why would you need to be caught?"

She rolled her eyes, acting like what I was saying was so ridiculous.

"*Relax.*"

"You weren't saying that back there in the store," I reminded her. "You told me to run."

"Okay, so what's the big deal? We didn't do anything. We left. What? Are we going to get arrested *for running out of a store*?" She groaned. "You know what? You are really messing up my mind right now."

I could sense that things were going to get real tense between us if I kept going, so I decided not to say anything else. Raq, however, surprisingly wouldn't let up.

"Always thinking with your mind." She *tsk-tsk*ed. "It's not gonna get you anywhere in life, *chica*. Might work for books and those damn tests you're always acing, but trying to do the smart thing, the right thing, all the damn time isn't gonna get you nothing but stay-at-home-with-Gramma boredom for the rest of your life. All right?"

With that, she turned over and flopped on her back.

But at least I won't have to run out of stores, I thought.

After a while she said, "Last summer, I saw this thing on the news, right? I was living in 'Nati still . . . This guy had a credit-card machine . . . Like, he was so good he could *make* credit cards, *chica*! It was crazy wild. But anyhow, it was nine years before they caught him. Nine *years*! And you know what he got?" She sat up and looked at me again, all animated and thrilled by the thought. "A shitload of fines. And that's it. Okay, so really, you think they're gonna care about some random kids trying to buy potato chips and a toy or two? *Chica* . . ." She offered me a look of pity.

I was afraid to ask but I had to. "So it was a stolen card, Raq?" I grimaced. "Are you serious? You cannot be serious!"

She laughed. "You're so funny . . ."

Who did the card really belong to? Was this the first one she'd stolen? Oh my goodness. Had she done this before? I didn't want to ask—I was too scared to hear what she might say. Instead, I closed my eyes for a moment, took a deep breath, and just asked her what time I should set the alarm for. I just wanted to go to sleep and deal with this tomorrow. Or, better yet, I wanted to wake up and pretend it hadn't even happened.

"Plus," she added, ignoring my question, "who really cares? At the end of the day, like Piper said, it's all just *dirt*."

And then, "On top of that, they have no idea who we even

are or how to find us. It's not like *my* name was on the card."

We. And how to find *us*? Was she serious? I hadn't stolen anything. Nor would I ever. She was out of her mind if she thought I was going to ride or die on that road.

"By the way," I told her, "Gee seemed suspicious when we got in the car. I caught a look in his eyes . . . In the rearview . . ."

She smacked her lips. "Please. That fool's just in love with me. He was probably trying to catch a glimpse."

"Maybe," I said, "but I still kinda think he knew something was up."

"It's all about perception, *chica*. Welcome to entertainment. Shit. Welcome to *life*."

"What?" I had no idea what she was talking about.

She rolled her eyes and laughed. "So, like, what in the world would you do without me to explain these things to you? What I'm saying is things are never what they seem. All of it. The glamour . . ."

She got up and started pacing around the room like she was a teacher, like she was giving me some kind of lesson. "Look at you." She gestured at my hoodie. "The *glitz* . . . What's that old saying about all the stuff that glitters ain't really gold? I mean, come on. You think Piper's fans realize right now that that fool is crashing at a Holiday Inn somewhere in Pittsburgh, trying to push it up the turnpike to do a show to chase a few dollars and some screams? Would *we* have thought that? Hell, no! We'd have thought he'd be on a first-class flight somewhere. Mun is the only one eating off all of this right now, *chica*, when you really think about it."

Part of me wanted her to just shut up. What did that have to do with what we had just been discussing? She was talking about everything in the world except stealing, which was so grimy. How could she?

She grunted. "We gotta believe it first. Then we gotta work to get it by any means necessary. Then we gotta act as *if* we're already what we want to be so the world will get the impression that we're already large. I'm just willing to do what I gotta do to start looking my part. You feel me?"

"Yeah," I said. I'd heard enough and didn't want to encourage her to continue. "Sounds great." I set the alarm for eight o'clock, then punched the pillow and tried to get comfortable. But inside I felt terrible. I always thought Raq and I had so much in common, that we saw the world the exact same way. But obviously we didn't.

◻ ◼ ◻

The alarm went off Monday morning before I even realized that I'd fallen asleep.

I peeked across the room. Raq wasn't in bed.

The bathroom door was open and the light wasn't on.

I heard a random *drip* of water and I sat up in bed, trying to focus my eyes.

What if she left me?

Where will I go?

What if they all left me?

But the overstuffed Target bag was still on her bed, so she must be around somewhere. Maybe talking to Gee, like yesterday morning.

And then . . .

Bizzzzzzzzz. Bzzzz. Bzzzzzzzzzzzzzzzzzzzzz.

Raq's phone was vibrating on the nightstand.

Bizzzzzzzzz. Bzzzz. Bzzzzzzzzzzzzzzzzzzzzz.

Gramma. I knew it.

As long as she hears your voice, she'll know you're fine, I could hear Raq say. So I answered.

"Hello?" I said.

A high pitched voice screamed. *"Raquel! Donde en el mundo es usted? Nosotros tan hemos sido preocupados!"*

"No, no," I said. "This is not Raquel."

The woman speaking gasped. *"No? Quién es esto?"*

"Lo siento," I said. *"Mi español es muy mal."*

"No?" she said. "So who is this? Ann?"

"Uh . . ."

"Hello? Where's Raquel?"

"I, uh . . ."

"Okay, listen, this is Kitty Ramirez—"

Whoa.

"Okay," I said. "I'll tell Raq you—"

"Please!" she shrieked. "Oh, *por favor*, don't hang up!"

I waited.

"Please," she said. "Just tell me, is she okay?"

I didn't answer.

"Please just . . . *sí* or *no* . . . Is she there?"

"I'll . . . um . . . I'll tell her to call you . . . Okay?"

"Is she all right?"

"Yes," I said. "She is."

"Oh, sweet Mary! Thank you. I've been so sick. She said she and her friend Ann were going to the party at school and after that she was spending the night at Ann's. Then my husband got a call that the car was left abandoned at some hall where a rap concert . . . And then Ann's grandmother has now called."

"Ma'am," I said, "I promise. I'll tell her you—"

"And then . . . *Mi hermano* . . . Credit cards reported missing from his store—"

Click. I hung up the phone.

So Raq had stolen a credit card from work! But wait, had Kitty said "cards," as in more than one? Oh my goodness . . .

Just then I heard the *click-click* of the door unlocking and Raq came sashaying in. Standing at the foot of my bed, she dumped out the contents of a Holiday Inn plastic laundry bag. There were a couple of high-end belts—a purple D&G and a Louis Vuitton—and two pairs of designer shades. There were also two jazzy-looking camisoles, one of them black lace and the other a black-and-silver zebra print. Lastly there was a pair of black leather pants. Already, Raq was peeling off her jeans and preparing to transform into a hottie. After buttoning up the pants, which hugged her in all the necessary places, she pulled on the black-and-silver camisole and then added the D&G belt and designer shades.

"Raq! Where in the world did you get all this stuff?"

She shrugged before going over to her bag to retrieve the black stilettos she had worn to the Halloween Jam. "It was almost *too* easy. Just watched for some fly mama to go to the workout room, swiped a housekeeper's key, and voilà. Took me all of four minutes," she said.

I sat jaw-locked.

She chuckled. "Took a shower before I left this morning, *chica*. I could've swiped from *you* if you had anything, you were so knocked out." She let out a hearty laugh. "I checked on Gee and Pipe. They said to meet them at the truck at noon."

I stared at all of the stolen goods. First the credit card, and now this?

"*Chica*," she said, excited. "Hurry up and shower. Try on

your new belt and stuff. Your *Glitz* hoodie will look good with that black lace tank. Come on!"

Great, my best friend was a klepto. Sure, I wanted to wear all those things—oh my goodness, they were nice—but this wasn't the way I'd imagined we would make a come-up in life. No way.

But what was I going to do? Call Gramma and say "Come get me. Oh, and by the way, I'm in Pennsylvania!"?

Raq said. "I hope you're not over there getting all goody on me. It's not a big deal, and it's time you started recognizing that this is real life. You talk about being babied by your grandmother and how she shelters you all the time but yet you act like you're afraid to bend your neck out and see what life is all about, all the stuff that she's trying to keep you from enjoying. Sometimes, if you really want something in this world—your dreams or whatever else—you gotta just go after it and *take it*. Once you do, it's yours. Ready for the world, right, *preemie baby*?" She winked and then smiled at me like she was so proud.

Then she added, "You're not gonna fade out on me, are you?"

No. Of course not. I'd come too far to turn back now. So Raq had another side I'd never seen before. There were probably things about me she didn't know either. And besides, *I* hadn't done the stealing. I wondered if in God's eyes all sins were the same.

Who would be more guilty—Raq for stealing? Or me for benefiting from her thefts?

As we left the hotel room shortly before noon, me in my lace camisole, skinny jeans, heels from Target, and guilty eyes, I carried my *Glitz* hoodie in hand and realized that I'd never felt so awful or looked so good. I decided not to even mention Kitty's phone call. I already knew what Raq would say. *Forget her,* chica*! Phony parents . . .*

13

Piper came out of the hotel looking more like a college guy than a hip-hop star. He wore a white button-down and baggy khakis and I recognized the tiny logo on his shirt. Expensive. His skin was freshly smoothed from lotion, his braids well-oiled, and his tiny sideburns razor-edged. His smile produced a bit of a dimple in his cheek, something I'd never noticed, as he approached. As he walked toward us it felt—for a second—like he was going to come over and hug me.

But when he got closer to the car, he looked Raq up and down then back up again. "Yo . . ." He grinned his approval of her tight leather pants.

Raq feigned a blush. "What's up, Pipe?" And then she made a production out of flipping her hair off her shoulder.

Gee was right behind Piper. He wore jeans, a white T-shirt, and clean work boots. With a small brown hairbrush in his hand, he was still grooming as he walked. His dark eyes offered immediate support of Raq's choice in clothes, too.

From my peripheral, I noticed a white police car cruising the lot, but I chose to ignore it. I was too focused on Piper's and Gee's reaction to Raq. For the most part, I was used to it. She *was* beautiful, and I knew that. But was I really that invisible?

Piper's hand—fingernails noticeably and newly well filed—was outstretched as he playfully waited to shake Raq's. The second before their palms touched, he nodded. "Yo . . ." he said. "You look so familiar. Didn't I see you in a fashion magazine?"

Gee laughed. "You stupid, Pipe . . ."

Raq giggled all cutesy and giddy-like.

As the police car cruised past again, I slipped on my rhinestone shades. Then I created a mantra and let it play over and over again in my mind. *Be tough. Be tough. Be cool. Be cool.*

Be Glitz.

"We better get going," I cheerfully reminded Sir Gee. "The road awaits us. . . ."

He laughed a quiet *yeah, you're right* laugh and unlocked the doors.

Glitz wouldn't have an attitude about Raq getting all the attention. She'd be over it. Nothing's gonna stop her fun.

We went to a McDonald's drive through for lunch—Piper's

treat—and Raq made small talk as we waited in the line. "So Pipe," she asked, "you never answered my question. You gonna let me get onstage with you in New York, or what?"

"Yo . . . you wearing them pants if I do?"

"You know it . . ." Raq sang playfully.

I slid down farther in my seat and eyed my hoodie on my lap. A moment later, I unzipped it, slipped it on, and covered every inch of my camisole's lace.

After we'd picked up our Big Macs from the window, Sir Gee pulled over in the parking lot and started dialing his phone. He put it on speaker and we all sat and waited for whoever he was calling to pick up.

"Speak!" a familiar voice barked.

"What up, Mun?"

"Paper. Tryna stack it. *What?* Any word on Cyn?"

"Yeah," Gee said. "Talked to Dana last night and again this morning. He's in stable condition. He'll be all right."

"Good." And then Mun-E's impatience was a loud silence. "Now, *what?*"

"Yo . . ." Piper smiled and shook his head, laughing at Mun's rudeness. "Me and Gee wanted to holla at you about that 'Liar, Liar' joint."

Silence.

Sir Gee said, "Mun? You there?"

"I'm listening. SPEAK!"

Gee continued, "This cute-assed dime, right? She got pipes. It's like something I never heard before."

Raq gasped and my eyes bucked. We grabbed each other's hands and squeezed. Suddenly, I felt silly for having been mad at Raq. This really could be her dream coming true. If she made it, she would have a chance to make right the things she'd done wrong, like stealing. Then this trip really would be worth it. I wanted so bad to be able to prove that to Gramma.

Piper nodded. "And yo . . . I heard her, too, Mun. Got mad soul. Maybe we could spin her at the Apollo. That'd be dope. . . ."

I heard Mun-E's breathing. "Whose idea was this? Callin' me with this bullshit—"

"Yo . . ." Piper interjected, "Mun. You just gotta trust me—"

Mun-E laughed. "Trust? Comedians on the line today, I see . . . I trust *no man*. Only God."

Sir Gee leaned back in his seat and started brushing his hair again. His eyes flinched with annoyance, but he chilled nonetheless.

Raq held my hand even tighter and then twisted her lips, holding back a smile. Mun-E said, "Where is she?"

Piper turned and looked directly at Raq. He winked. "Gee, go grab her real quick. . . ."

Sir Gee looked up into the rearview, linked eyes with Raq,

and—cupping his mouth like a megaphone—yelled, "Ay, *Raq*! Come holla at Pipe for a minute." Then he held up his fist and blinked the countdown. Five . . . Four . . . Three . . . Two . . . One . . . He pointed at Raq and nodded. She was on.

"What up, Pipe?" Raq winced and then took a deep breath.

"Yo . . ." Pipe nodded his approval. "I got my mans on the phone, right? You wanna get that hook up for the Jam-Master Jay tribute? Ya gotta let him know."

"That's what's up," she said. Then she looked at me.

I slipped my hand from hers and put both of mine together.

Lord, if you can hear me. Please just give her a chance.

I'd never seen someone want something so bad before in my life. And Raq deserved it, especially after all she'd been through in her life.

She closed her eyes and gave it all the heart she had beating inside of her. And when she sung it that time, believe me, the hook had never sounded so strong. Halfway through, Sir Gee was nodding his head and Piper was pumping his fist.

Thank you, God.

Thank you . . .

When Raq was finished, we all held our breath until Mun spoke. "I'll get back to you." *Click.*

Raq and I screamed.

Then, we looked at each other. Waited a second . . .

Then we screamed again. Louder this time.

Sir Gee and Piper were up front laughing and giving each other dap.

He hadn't said *no*. And that's all that mattered in that moment.

Mun-E.

Hadn't.

Said.

No.

Raq was one giant step closer to singing hook with Piper. And when it happened, I was gonna be there with her, to hold her up, to cheer her on, to make sure she didn't crack under pressure. But of course she wouldn't. She was Raquel Marissa Diaz. Anyone who'd ever seen her knew she was extraordinary. And anybody who ever heard her sing knew she was destined.

"Thank you, Piper," she said.

"Yo . . ." Piper said, "Piper knows a gift when he hears it."

Gee drove as we ate, and I considered something. What if Piper had been a jerk when we met him? Or arrogant? Or rude? What if he had told Gee no when we wanted to come into the dressing room after the concert, or after that when we wanted to hop along in that SUV? A million what-ifs played in my mind, but the bottom line was that everything *had* happened. And now, Raq was closer than ever to her dreams.

And I was farther away from home than I'd ever meant to be.

✠ ✠ ✠

It was a five-hour drive from Pittsburgh to Philadelphia, so we got into the city late in the afternoon.

Gee was used to Philly and easily navigated the narrow and winding hills, past cars parked in the medians, and landed us in Merion Township, according to the signs I'd seen as we pulled into the parking lot for the King of Prussia Mall. I'd never seen anything like it. It was at least seven times bigger than Westfield Franklin Park back home.

Raq and I were standing underneath the massive shopping center's glass-domed ceiling, taking in all of the grandness. I imagined that it was like being in the lobby of a really fancy hotel, only the mall was full of stores instead of rooms. It looked like there was something for everyone, from high-end shops to trendy little boutiques to regular mall stores, an easy blend of offerings for the privileged, the working class, and us dreamers.

Piper treated us to the Cheesecake Factory for dinner—I had a shrimp po'boy and fries—and we toasted to being in "The City of Brotherly Love" with milkshakes, then we agreed to meet up in a couple of hours. We were *supposed* to be discreetly slipping free CDs into the hands of anyone we saw who looked like they dug hip-hop. Piper said it was called "grassroots marketing" and necessary for independent record labels wanting to expand their reach.

Most malls have strict no-soliciting laws, Piper said, but

technically we weren't selling anything, we were just giving things away. Gee warned us, though, that if mall security approached us, we should just be polite and make our exit. But after forty-five minutes my backpack was still loaded down with CDs—I kept offering them to people but they kept shaking their heads no—and Raq was thinking aloud about where to shop. I wanted to help support Piper, of course, but we were both more fascinated with the mall itself.

"I'm thinking we'll start with The Icing," she decided. "We should definitely find you some new jewelry, *chica*."

There it was, the awful heaviness in my stomach I had felt this morning after Raq lifted that stuff from the woman at the hotel. I knew she'd mentioned having cash, but now I was wondering how she'd even gotten that. Was it stolen too?

Well, she did have a job, I reasoned. *Up until Saturday. So maybe this was money she had earned.*

I followed Raq's casual pace through the mall. We made stops at various stores—just peeking and glancing—and stopped to fantasize like the tourists we were at the Cartier window. Raq leaned in closer to me, the light from the diamonds glistening on her face, and she said two words: "One day . . ."

We stopped in the Puma store, and Raq picked up a pair of white-on-white wristbands. "Let's get these for Piper," I said.

"He'd love them," she agreed. They were on sale for nine dollars. Before Raq could do it, I paid for them myself. She didn't protest, and I was glad. After tax I had less than ten dollars, but at least I'd bought something for Piper.

"By the way," she said as we strolled, "I've been wondering . . . Are you digging on Piper?"

"What?" I said. "His music?"

She nudged me. "Come on . . ."

I nudged her back. "What?"

"Be honest," she said.

I took a deep breath. "I don't know. Maybe . . . A little. But what'd be the point?" I watched for her reaction. I never told her what he'd said about her back at the Waffle House, but surely she could see the way he'd been looking at her.

Raq started to laugh so hard, she had to stop walking, causing an old man with a cane to almost bump into her.

"What?" I stood there watching as she didn't bother to apologize to the man.

"I'm sorry," she said to me, and wiped her eyes, which had begun to water up from her laughing so hard.

"What's so damn hilarious?" I asked.

"Picture Piper . . . having a girlfriend"—she shook her head—"when all he cares about is music. Please."

On one hand my feelings were hurt. On the other, I knew she was right. Of course Piper wouldn't want me to be his steady girl, but why wasn't such a thing worthy of grandiose, seemingly impossible imagining, too?

She said, "You're so gullible, it's cute."

"Excuse me?" I completely stopped walking. "'Gullible'?"

"Forget it." She kept walking. "Come on . . . Don't stand there looking all wounded like that. I was just kidding."

"I must've missed the joke, then," I said. "Ha. Ha."

A few awkward moments later she announced, "You've got so much to learn. . . ."

"What *now*?" I asked.

Ignoring my irritated tone, she said, "First of all, the key to getting a man to do anything is to make them want you physically. Once they chase after your goods, they will do whatever you want. Now, officially, you can't let them know you are getting them to do what you want—their egos are too huge—but it's jackpot for you if you play your cards right. Watch and learn from me, *chica*. Got it?"

I just looked at her. Not only was Raq not making any sense, she sounded stupid.

"Whatever," I said. "Let's just unload these CDs."

"Yeah, I guess we should," she said, pulling a CD out of her bag to look at it. There was Buckstarr's name, right there under Piper's. "But right here it says 'Buckstarr' when it should say 'Raq.' And to me, that's a problem."

"Okay . . ."

"Let me see that backpack," she demanded.

I slipped the straps from my shoulders and handed it to her. She pulled her shades out of her purse and slid them on for effect. Then she eased my bag over a metal trash can and dumped in all of Piper's CDs. Just like that.

"See, *chica* . . . I'm laying bricks, building the house of Raquel Marissa Diaz. I keep playing my cards right and Piper will be like an itty-bitty penny in the palm of my hand. That fool loves me. He just doesn't know it yet." She handed my bag back to me, empty and light now.

"I can't believe you just did that." I looked over at the trash can. How could she do that to Piper, after all he had done for us?

She looked stunned. "Why not?"

I shook my head. "Raq, you just threw away a bag full of Piper's promo CDs. It's the reason we're here in the first place. We're supposed to be—"

"All right!" She threw her hand up. And then she lowered her voice. "I guess I'm just gonna need to know whose side you're really on. Right now."

"Huh? Why would I need to chose between you and Piper?"

"That's not it," she said. It's me"—she paused—"or Buckstarr."

Oh.

She nodded when she saw that I was following her train of thought now.

She said, "Because if you think I'm going to walk this mall pushing another chick's dream"—she chuckled— "then you don't know Raquel Marissa Diaz."

I couldn't help a quick chuckle. Raq was so relentless. "You're crazy," I said.

"Thanks, *chica.*" She smiled.

◻ ◼ ◻

We spent an hour in Forever 21 trying on clothes and Raq dropped almost a hundred bucks on dresses for both of us.

Handing me my bag, she said, "FYI, Gee said Mun's talking about latching them on Millionaire Mal's *Inked and Paid* tour. That'd be hot, huh? Piper would be all up in the mainstream after that. . . ."

I zipped my hoodie up all the way to my chin, let my bags rest on my arms, and stuffed my fists in my pocket. "Good for him," I said.

She flipped her hair. "You should have seen Gee this morning. You were still asleep when I ran into him in the hallway. He was all over me. Like he wanted to eat me alive." She laughed and then pulled her hair up in the back. "Did he mark me?"

Sure enough there was a blush-red love mark on the back of her neck.

"Nope," I said, full knowing that Raq had probably already been all up in the mirror this morning. Really, she just wanted *me* to see it. "It looks like a rash," I said.

"Yeah, right." She let her hair fall back down. "I hope I didn't mark him, too. Guys hate that."

First she was talking about Piper, about how he loved her and didn't know it yet, and now she was talking about Gee again? So she had to have them *both*? Or was it just that she didn't want me to have either one?

⧅ ⧆ ⧅

In the parking lot, we walked up on Piper and Gee standing by the truck. Two blonde girls were giggling like hyenas as Piper autographed CDs for them. Both girls were in six-inch heels and designer duds, and it looked like they shopped on the daily.

Raq said "Damn groupies" under her breath, but kept stepping.

The two girls noticed us approaching and reacted to something Piper said that we couldn't hear. Then they both looked to be suppressing a giggle.

"Bye, Piper MC . . . Bye, Sir Gee . . ." one of them said, both of them waving as they walked away and not bothering to look at either of us as they passed.

Gee spotted the bags Raq and I were carrying. "I see y'all havin' fun on your little spree." He took Raq's bags and put them in the trunk next to the remaining boxes of CDs we were supposed to be giving out on the road.

Piper reached out and took my bags, too. Our hands touched when he did. "What up, Glitz?" He smiled.

I checked my peripheral. Was Raq watching me? Sure enough, she was.

"Nothing much," I said, reaching in to fumble around in the Puma bag. "I bought you something. . . ."

"*We* saw them and instantly thought of you," Raq said.

He smiled at Raq when he saw them. *"Yo . . ."* And slipped them right on.

The way he looked at her then, it was as if I could read his mind in that moment: *Glitz, who?*

Sometimes you just gotta wait your turn, Raq told me once.

And so I wondered, *Will mine ever come?* For anything?

14

When I was a little girl, more than anything I just wanted to make Gramma proud. And most of the time I did. Stars and smiley faces on my papers. Praise from my teachers on my midterm reports. Never got in any trouble, not even so much as detention. I really tried hard to be good. And I succeeded.

Now I was on the run.

On Tuesday morning, when I should have been going to school, I woke up in the Courtyard Marriott on Juniper Street in downtown Pennsylvania, surrounded by intimidating buildings, too much traffic, and probably dozens of police completely unaware of the delinquents resting on the eighth floor.

For once, Raq was still in bed, sleeping. She looked so harmless that I could have laughed. She must have sensed me waking up, because soon she stirred.

Her voice soft and sleepy, she smiled and stretched when she saw me. "Ay, *chica . . .*"

"Hey," I replied, curling up in bed with a sigh.

Last night, before we'd gone to bed, I had given Raq the okay to push Gramma's phone calls through to voice mail. But I woke up thinking about her anyway.

"She called four times, at least," Raq said, reading my mind.

Whatever. There was no way I could call her back. I'd passed the point of reasoning with her. If she heard my voice now, a surge of fire would definitely burst through the phone.

We'd agreed to get an early start passing out CDs that day, and I grabbed a postcard and a stamp from the gift shop on our way out for the day.

> Dear Gramma,
> Sorry if I hurt you or made you worry.
> I love you. And I am . . . O.K.
> P.S. Raq's really got something!
> Someday I'll play her CD for you.
> You'll tap your toes like it's Natalie Cole . . .
> And maybe you'll understand . . .
> xoxo—Glitz

I dropped it in a box near where we stood in downtown Philadelphia on the corner of Market Street and Fifteenth. In full *Glitz* mode, I put on my shades, zipped up my hoodie, and pulled up the hood. It was a little chilly outside now, and while Gee and Piper were a couple of blocks over, stopping schoolkids as they walked toward the SEPTA bus stop, me and Raq had positioned ourselves to pass out CDs to random passersby. The goal was to drop as many CDs on the road to New York as possible.

"What kind of music is it?" a scholarly looking Asian woman asked as she took the CD I was holding out to her. She tightened the hood on her windbreaker.

"Rap," I replied.

She read the title on the CD and looked puzzled. "Monster?"

The wind made me shiver. "Do you know any teenagers?"

She nodded.

"Just give it to 'em." I shivered some more. "They'll love it. Trust me."

She still looked confused but went on her way, Piper's CD in hand.

A couple of hours later, when Raq had just been standing there chatting it up with some random guy who approached her, I had given away an entire stack of CDs. Needing to refresh my supply, I waved to get her attention. I could tell she still had plenty.

"Be right back," I said.

Raq kept talking with the thugged-out-looking hottie, but she threw up her hand and smiled to let me know she'd heard me.

I crossed blocks, getting an occasional bump from a fellow rushed pedestrian, until I spotted the Hummer. Gee was standing in front of it, talking to a couple of goofy-looking girls with plaid uniforms peeking out from underneath their jackets. It reminded me of school. I don't think I'd ever so much as been tardy, and here I was totally skipping. When I got back home, I promised myself, I was going to dive right back into the books and be my studious self again. I had to.

Piper was busy signing CDs at the back of the truck for some boys on skateboards. He looked up when he saw me standing there and gave me a quiet smile, raising his wrist up in the air as a reminder of his appreciation for the gift. "Yo . . ."

"Hey, Piper," I said with a smile. "Just back for another stack."

After the kids walked away with their CDs, Piper reached into the back of the truck and handed me a bunch more.

"I need a break," he said, leaning against the side of the truck.

I wasn't too eager to get back to watch Raq flirt with strangers and toss CDs in the trash instead of giving them away, so I also decided to take a break, too. I leaned back against the truck beside Piper and—by accident—positioned myself too close. Our shoulders touched. He didn't move, though, when it happened. So I didn't move either. We both watched the hustling streets of downtown Philadelphia. But for me, it was as if all the traffic was on mute. All I could hear were my own heartbeats in my ears.

"Appreciate the help," he said. "With the CDs . . ."

"A lot of folks said they'd heard of you, you know. When I gave them the CD. . . ."

"That's how you swell. . . . Gotta touch locals. . . . Locals grow to states. States grows to mainstream. Grassroots. It's what we do."

I laughed. "They're like, 'Piper MC? I know him! He was at the park,' or, 'He was at the Illadelph Legends Festival. . . .'"

"Yo . . ." His smile was proud. "I stay grindin', ya dig? Got to."

"It's more than just your grind though, Piper. It's your music. People love it. And you make us think, too. It's amazing. . . ."

"Just searchin' like the next good man," he said. "Music's my map."

I wondered what he meant by that—his map—but I decided to just keep listening.

He said, "Tryna find the answers . . . The reasons . . . The messengers. The *messages* . . ."

He looked off into the sky like something—maybe the answer or the reason or the messenger or the message—was sitting on a cloud somewhere. Like he could just reach out and pick it up. I resisted the urge to look up and reach right out with him.

The worst thing in the world, Piper told me then, was to be content.

He said, "The man with power is not the man with all the dirt," he said. "It's the man who stays *searching. . . .*"

"Really?"

"Yo . . ." He tapped his chest. "That's heart talk."

"What do you mean?" I asked.

"Means that's real talk, that's all. My mans Terry Lewis said, '*What comes from the heart, speaks to the heart.*'" He reached over and touched my arm. "Follow me?"

"Yeah," I said. "I do."

"You're a smart girl." He let his arm fall back to his side. "So you tell me what it means. The one searching, why does Glitz think that's the most powerful person in the world?"

I thought for a moment. "Because the one searching is the one who finds . . ."

". . . all the answers." His smile was proud. "Yo, you got it. See, some people stumble upon knowledge, but they don't appreciate that gold because they weren't looking for it. Some people don't even give a damn, so they walk right over it. But the ones searching . . ." He rubbed his hands together as if the idea was suddenly new and exciting to him.

He said, "I can tell a lot about you, Glitz. You look for the meanings in things . . . the reasons . . . Not everybody can do that. Not everybody wants to. Some people can only see the surface, ya dig?" He looked at me in a new way, like he was really hoping I was listening. I was. "Stay thirsty," he said and then tapped his heart.

"I will," I promised.

⌑ ◪ ⌑

That evening, Raq was pacing the hotel room and calling Piper and Sir Gee all kinds of curse words in Spanish. We'd been pushing free CDs all day and they'd dropped us at the hotel afterward, saying that they were running down to Applebee's to grab some eats and would bring food back for all of us.

Never one to sweat a guy, Raq had simply replied, "Okay," and noted what she wanted from the restaurant. I had done the same. But now, four hours had passed. It was nearly ten o'clock.

Just as Raq screamed in frustration, her phone began to vibrate.

She picked it up from the bed and rolled her eyes at the caller ID. "Here"—she tossed me the phone—"answer it." "She's been calling every hour. And I do mean *every*. I'm sick of it."

Without thinking, I answered. "Hi, Gramma," I said.

Her voice was a hurried panic. "Where-are-you?" She definitely sounded ticked *and* worried.

"I'm fine."

"Fine! What on God's blessed earth has possessed your tormented little mind, child?"

"Gramma," I said, "please. Don't! The important thing is that I'm—"

She gasped. "You little heathen! I've called the police, the fire department, Blockwatch, the FBI, Anderson Cooper, Geraldo Rivera, Nancy Grace—"

"Gramma!"

"Yes. I. *Did*. Calling the police again, too. As long as you're alive I'm gonna need them to stop me from killing you. Nothing—"

"Did you hear what you just said? I can't believe you would—"

"I know what I said! Words came from my mouth, didn't they?" she interjected. "You just better hope you're gonna survive this ass whoopin' you got comin'."

Gramma hadn't spanked me since I was probably eight years old—hollering and fussing was her belt of choice most days—but today I wasn't so sure she wouldn't actually do it when I made it home.

She said, "How are you even eating? Oh God . . . *What* are you eating? Don't eat *nothing* that child cooks!"

"I'm eating fine. . . ."

"I bet you are! The Ramirezes said that child walked away with twelve hundred dollars. Cash. Y'all little rascals are probably eatin' lobster."

I looked over at Raq. She was staring out the window. "Really?" I said.

"Look at her real good. You can see writing right there in her eyes. Left one says BAD and right one says NEWS. Judge said they're washing their hands of it. Of *her.* As much as they tried to help that girl, and that little wicked child stole money from them? Kitty's brother said she got away with three people's credit cards, too."

Twelve hundred dollars, I thought. Man. Raq had more cash than she'd let on. And it was stolen. Maybe she did worship the devil. Maybe she *was* the devil.

Raq was still pacing, caring only about the whereabouts of Piper and Gee.

Gramma continued, "Out there lollygagging like you're grown. Like you think you can just do what you want to do. That little heathen child don't care about anything, but you know better. You were raised better than this. Where are you? Downtown somewhere? The Old West End? The mall? Get home *now.*"

"Gramma," I said, "I'm okay. And I'll be home soon. Okay?"

"What!" she shouted. "You think you can just *tell me* when you'll be home? You've missed two days of school. Child, I'm embarrassed to even ask people to pray for you. You know what that's like having to go before an entire congregation and have to report that your grandchild has become an *idiot*? Tell me where you are right *now*. I'm coming to get you. You're going to school tomorrow!"

I sighed.

Gramma continued, "Oh, if I could just snatch you through this phone I would wring your neck! I told you that girl was trouble! I shoulda rebuked her the first time I laid eyes on her. Your mother and your father—rest their blessed souls—would be so hurt, you out there acting like this. Like you don't have home training. I'm gonna snatch you when I see you! Promise you that!"

I fell back on the bed and groaned.

Gramma spoke through her teeth. "All my life . . . All I've sacrificed for you . . ."

"Gram—"

"Naw, naw. You need to hear this. I've bended and folded every part of my soul just to pick up where your mama and your daddy couldn't—God rest their blessed souls—and this is what I get?"

Then she shrieked, "Lord! Why? . . . Why? . . . Father, *whyyy?* . . ."

I could hear her crying, and this choked me a bit. "Gramma . . . Gramma please don't cry."

Raq walked back and forth, sucking her teeth and rolling her eyes. She gulped a generous amount of the ginger ale she had gotten from the vending machine as I was talking.

"Really," I said, "Gramma, I don't think you should be so upset. I'm okay . . ."

She sniffed and her voice sounded drained. "Goodness. Gracious. For the love of *God*—"

"Gramma," I said, "I'll call you—"

"Call me!" she shouted.

My head throbbing with tension now, I said, "Gramma, I can't . . ."

"Can't? You must be rabbit mad, child. Telling me what you *can't do.*"

My knuckles began making impatient music on the nightstand. *Tap-tap. Tap-tap. Tap-tap.* "*Gramma*," I said after a few more taps, "I'll call you tomorrow."

"What do you mean, you'll call me to—"

I pushed END on the phone and tossed it onto the bed, wondering why I'd even bothered answering it in the first place. It hadn't done any good. Maybe what I really needed to do was keep stepping and never look back. For the rest of my life she was going to keep fussing and trying to control me. Life had to be better than this.

After snatching the phone from the bed, Raq fumbled around with the buttons and dialed on speaker. A ripple of relief passed over her face as someone finally answered on the other end.

"Yo . . ."

She had his phone number now! Since when? I couldn't believe it.

"What's up, Piper!" Raq took a breath. "We were starting to worry."

"Hold on a second," he said. It was hard to understand what he was saying to someone else, but we could hear his voice and other voices, too. And I could see rage brewing in Raq's eyes.

What would happen to us if Gee and Piper just left us here?

What if they were sick of us and were somewhere rolling with the two blonde chicks they'd met at the mall?

Finally, Gee got on the phone. "Whaddup?"

"My quesadilla burger, fool," Raq quipped. "*That's* what's up."

Gee laughed. "My bad, ma. Mun got us linked on that Millionaire tour starting next week. Over here at Kinko's, waitin' on a fax, tryna see it official."

Raq's face softened. "For real? That's tight."

"Yeah . . . So, be easy. We'll be there in a few."

"All right, then," she said. "Cool."

Raq hung up and looked at me, wide-eyed and ready to scream. "Did you hear that!"

"Whoa," I said.

"Piper's *really* about to explode."

"To say the least . . ."

"We *gotta* stay in with him."

"Whip-tee," I said. "Maybe I should use your phone again? Let Gramma know I'm going on tour now. . . ." I looked away. Inside I was on the verge of crying. Of course I wanted to go on tour with Piper, too. But what Gramma had told me about the money Raq stole from the Ramirezes, and the stolen credit cards, too . . . I hated to admit—I couldn't admit—but this wasn't feeling so cool. And wow. Raq might get to go on tour with Piper and Gee and Millionaire Mal while I stayed home with Gramma tucking me in at night. *"Chica,"* she sounded as if she pitied me. "You're not gonna live your whole life for her. Don't even sweat it."

"I know . . ."

"Didn't I tell you . . . As long as you let her hear your voice, she'll stay in check? That's all you gotta do. *Gramma, I'm fine.* And then hang up. She doesn't have to know where you are or when you're coming home. All that fussing she does is bluff. She'll say anything to make you hate me."

"Bluff? Raq! You have no idea. She's really upset."

And then, out of the blue, she said, "Gee is so annoying."

"Huh?" I literally looked around to see where our conversation had landed after she'd just tossed it away like that.

"Yeah," she said. "Wonder if he ever gets tired of being backup for Piper. Of being Mun's personal *yes-man.*" She leaned down, popped off her shoe, and scratched the bottom of her toe. "These stilettos are making me itch." She reached into her pocket, pulled out a spicy peppermint, and popped it out of its wrapper.

I found a stick of gum in my backpack and popped it in my mouth. I was about to explode and needed something else to do with my nerves, too. If Raq was going on tour with Piper, I deserved to be there, too. Maybe even instead of her. She hardly even bothered to help pass out CDs, which is what we were supposed to be doing with them on the road in the first place.

"What kills me," she said as she smacked and crunched, "is how he's always talking about doing it big when really Pipe is the man, you know? Ask me, Gee is nothing but a low-class thug in Piper's million-dollar game. I hate him." She laughed.

Then she said. "Have you noticed how Piper is always staring me down?"

I reminded her, "Well, if it weren't for Gee, *we* wouldn't be here. Don't forget that. You couldn't have just walked up and stepped to Piper that night, not the way you did with Gee."

Absentmindedly, I reached down and grabbed my backpack, gripping it like I was about ready to fall and needed the weight not to do so. I stared over at Raq. Again, she was scratching her toe. In that moment, I knew that there was no itch. She was up to something.

And that something was Piper.

When they finally got back with our food, Raq immediately gave Piper a hug.

"Congratulations," she said, bouncing up and down as she hugged him. "Piper, you are the *shit*! Mal isn't gonna know what hit that tour!"

Hugging her back, a tad awkwardly at first, Piper laughed. "Yo . . . that's what's up."

When Raq had finally loosened the grip around Piper's neck, I said from across the room, "You're the man, Pipe. Congratulations."

He nodded. "Appreciate that, Glitz."

Gee was pulling the plastic containers of food out of the bag and stopped to look over his shoulder. "Dang, can a brother get some love?" He laughed. "I'm going, too."

Raq shoved him playfully. "You know you're the man, Gee." She pulled his arm until he leaned down so she could deposit a kiss on his cheek.

I smiled at Gee, too. "Congratulations," I said.

As we ate, Raq was constantly flicking a speck of something off of Piper's shirt or brushing back one of his braids.

"So how many cities?" she asked him.

"Twenty-two."

"And when does it start?"

"Next week," Piper said. "Gotta definitely get back to

the D this Saturday. . . . We leave right back out again on Sunday."

"Wow . . ." Raq touched his arm. "I'm so happy for you, Piper. . . . We should celebrate."

Gee reached for the remote control and turned up the volume on an infomercial. "We plan to, tomorrow night."

Raq whispered to Piper.

Piper whispered back.

Raq laughed.

Piper laughed even louder.

I stared at Raq.

She didn't even look at me.

When Piper finished his food and got up, she got up, too.

What was I going to say? *No, you can't go with him?*

No, Piper, you can't leave with her?

Neither of them even said good-bye.

15

After Piper and Raq left the room, Gee just shrugged, took out his cell phone, and started texting. I made myself useful, cleaned up all the plastic containers of leftover food, stuffed them into the plastic bags, and wiped the table down. When I finished, Gee was stretched out on what was supposed to be Raq's bed.

I grabbed the remote control and, while flipping through the stations, I thought I saw Gramma on the screen. But no. It was just some other thin-framed educated-looking woman talking to Larry King on CNN, something about politics. I looked over at Gee, his back to me, a lump of silence.

I flicked off the television and turned on the radio instead.

Now it was officially Wednesday. 12:02 A.M.

Just after midnight. And I was definitely not feeling like Cinderella anymore.

I fumbled with the stations, trying to find one that was playing some good music.

One station was playing Millionaire Mal. I kept turning before it made me sad.

Wonder what Raq and Piper are talking about . . . Or if they are even talking at all . . .

Sir Gee stirred and turned to look at the radio, watching me turn from crackling sound to country jam to crackling sound to people talking.

"Try a ninety," he said.

"Huh?"

He cleared his throat, "If you stay in the nineties, you'll usually hit something in most cities. Point three . . . Point five . . . Point seven . . . Point nine. Something usually comes in."

And he was right. After a few turns in the nineties, I heard the familiar sounds of Usher, a throwback slow jam from his *Confessions* CD. I balled up the pillow and curled up under the covers as it played.

"Thanks." I sighed. "Never knew that."

"No prob." He turned his back to me once more. Moments passed and then he stirred again.

"Why you so quiet all the time?" he wanted to know. He was sitting up now.

"I'm not," I said. "Not really . . ."

"You always just have this look on your face, like you got something on your mind."

"Sometimes," I said, "maybe I do."

"You're different from your girl . . ." He tilted his head. "You're real sweet though, you know?"

He'd said it like I was a puppy dog or something.

I laughed. "Um, is that supposed to be a compliment?"

"For sure," he said. *"For sure."*

He stared some more.

Then he bit his bottom lip. "Kinda cute, too. . . ."

How he looked at me then was different from how he had before. His expression was more direct now, more focused, and I got a good look at his eyes for the first time. They were more intense than I'd realized.

He patted the bed. "Come here."

He wanted me to come *there.*

"For what?" I asked.

He kinda laughed. But he didn't smile. "Girl, quit actin' shy . . ." Then he said, "Wit' yo' cute self . . ."

I joined him on the bed but kept a space between us.

It felt like sitting next to a big old oak tree, Sir Gee was so big and solid.

He took my hand and rubbed it. His skin felt rough and dry.

As he massaged my fingertips, he watched my face.

I stared up at the ceiling, studying the water stains and trying to make sense of what was happening.

He kissed my neck, his lips hard and forceful. Once. And then again.

No way. This *couldn't* be right.

His breathing grew noticeably louder.

Then he began rubbing my arm.

I was fixed on the bed like a mound of leftover cooking grease.

Piper had only touched my arm and it had left a lifetime of tingles.

Nothing about Gee's touch felt good to me.

But I tried to lay back as he kissed my neck, my cheek . . .

He held my hand even firmer. Then he whispered into my ear. "Can I have you?"

There was no pretending. No way. No thank you. I deserved better.

I deserved Piper.

"I'm sorry," I said, sitting straight up. "I . . . I'm sorry, Gee."

He patted me just above my hip and chuckled.

Then his back was to me again.

◻ ◼ ◻

The next morning, Wednesday, Gee probably thought I was still asleep, that I hadn't heard him get up and shower, dress and, now, yak on the phone. But really I had been awake thinking for a while. I just wanted to avoid any awkwardness.

"We're on our way, Mun! How many times I gotta tell you that?"

Finally, I sat up in bed, flicked through the channels on the remote control, and kept my focus on the television where *The View* was on. The room was dim and tense, two people having awoken from a night of nothing but sleep. Too nervous to wear pajamas with just me and Gee in the room, I'd fallen asleep in my clothes. I wondered if Raq had felt the same way. In the next room. With Piper. From the corner of my eye, I saw Gee snatch open the ice bucket, toss a couple of watered-down cubes from last night into a glass from the bathroom, and then splash the contents of a tiny sample-size bottle of liquor on top of it. *Drinking so early in the morning?* I thought as he continued to fuss with Mun-E.

"All right, man. I can't get him to the interview if I'm on the phone with you." Then he hung up. I heard the clink of the ice in his glass as he slammed it on the table, the jingle of his keys, and then he noticed I was awake. His voice dry, he said, "You better get ready. Meet y'all out at the truck."

Relieved when the door closed behind him, I sprang out of bed.

All he had done was sleep, and yet I had never craved a shower so much in my life.

⋈ ⬧ ⋈

"Hey, *chica*." Raq climbed in the backseat beside me.

Like it was nothing.

Like it was all good.

"Hey," I replied, trying in vain to sound just as regular.

Seriously, how could things be the same after what had clearly happened between her and Piper last night? After I told her I liked him and she laughed at me? Now I knew why: She just wanted him for herself.

We remained silent as we rode along. Piper was scheduled for a local radio on-air interview at two thirty. Looking out the window at all the buildings in downtown Philly, I took a deep breath and tried to consume it all. The tall buildings, the people rushing around, all the taxis. But then a thought popped into my head: What if Gramma had really notified the authorities? And what if they found us?

Just then I thought I had my answer. A big blue light was shining from behind us.

Panic loaded into my chest.

"Yo . . ." Piper was sitting up front where he had been text messaging and suddenly he dropped his phone in his lap. "What we pushing?"

"I'm not speeding!" Gee replied, fishing around in his pocket for his driver's license before easing the truck into a gas station parking lot. I could see the expression on Gee's face as he checked the side view, the rearview. He grimaced when the patrol car crawled into the lot right behind us.

I closed my eyes and for the first time, I truly wished I could wake up from this dream.

Raq whipped a couple of credit cards from her purse and slipped them down into her cleavage. After that, she was cool. Not even an extra blink.

Standing at the car door was a police officer, his hair prematurely gray, his eyes weary as someone who'd been doing the same job too long.

Gee's voice was polite as he rolled down the window. "A problem, Officer?"

"Seventy-two, *at least*," the cop replied, sounding just like every voice I'd ever heard in every nightmare I'd ever had since I was five years old, since the first time I overheard Gramma telling someone about the night the police had come to the door to tell her about my parents' accident. Police, in my mind, only showed up to announce bad news.

Raq and I had pictured ourselves downing pricey champagne, laughing while tossing our heads back. Now, with Raq's stolen credit cards, stolen cash from Judge and Kitty, and the fact that we were runaways, I wondered if I would be spending the rest of my life behind bars.

Please God. Please don't let me go to jail.

Please don't let my life be over yet...

Gee cleared his throat, handed over his license and registration, and rolled up the window while the officer walked back to his patrol car. I tried to appear at ease, too, despite the whimper on the tip of my tongue.

I glanced at Raq. She might as well have been whistling out loud, her demeanor was so relaxed. Piper looked mellow, too.

It was all so unnerving, waiting forever in silence. I wanted to burst through the roof of the truck, hop out, and run back to Toledo. What in the world could that police officer possibly be back in his car doing?

Finally, I could see him approaching the side of the truck. He tapped on the window and waited for Gee to roll it down again. I let out a long breath as Gee put his finger on the button and the window hummed quietly on its way down.

The officer said, "What's the rush? Headed somewhere special?"

"No rush," Gee said.

Piper chimed in. "Just passing through town, Officer. On our way to Power 99, the radio station."

"I see . . ." the officer said, looking over everyone the car. "Gonna have to cite you for speeding."

"My bad, Officer." Gee's jawbones were pumping, but he sounded okay.

After he finished preparing the ticket, the officer handed Gee the citation. "Slow down. . . ."

In an agreeable tone unlike him, Gee looked straight ahead and replied, "Will do, Officer. Thank you."

As Gee rolled up the window and the officer walked away, I felt my entire body exhale. This was it. I *had* to get home. Forget New York. For the Apollo. Forget Raq. Forget—

"Yo . . ." Piper said, "Y'all all cool?"

Raq answered yes. I didn't say a word.

Piper looked at me. "Glitz? You a'ight?"

I was So. Not. Okay. "Sure," I said with a wimpy smile.

"Yo . . . Always gonna be something out there tryna taint a blessing. Always something gonna try and distract you, you know? When you're trying to do your thing . . . When it's somewhere you're trying to go, something you're trying to do in life . . . Focused. Gotta stay determined. Can't take your eyes off the goal."

Piper was right. I'd come so far and I at least wanted to be able to say I made it to New York. I at least wanted to have a glimpse of the Empire State Building. Just a little longer, and Glitz would be over. But while she was still here, I was determined to sit back and enjoy the ride.

⋈ ✖ ⋈

"Yo . . ." Piper was sitting across from Sienna Jax, a stylish young deejay dressed like a classy diva in a body-hugging sweater dress and with diamond studs in her ears.

"Thank you so much for being here with us, Piper," Sienna said.

Piper smiled at her. "It's my pleasure. Piper always listens to my girl Sienna Jax when I'm in Philly." He spun one of the keys on his keychain around and around. It was the first time I'd ever seen him fidget.

Me, Raq, and Gee stood off to the side watching the interview.

"You rap so much about pain," she said. "Why is that, Piper?"

"Pain?" he said. "I rap about *life.* You gotta understand, Ms. Sienna, *life* is like drivin' a Porsche in an ice storm, in below-zero temperatures. I'm lovin' it. Feels so good pushing something so fly, but that don't stop all the worrying, the fact that all around me people are crashing and I can't drive as free as I want 'cause there's so much that can eff up my ride. . . ."

Sienna raised her eyebrows, "Careful, brotha . . ."

"My apologies." Piper smiled. "But really . . . It's like constantly we wonder, what's up ahead? Is the road too slick? Is this ride gonna kill me? Will I get hurt? Hurt *again*, even."

Piper pressed his lips to the microphone and I noticed the way he held it, between two fingers and his thumb. And then he added, "I just come from the heart. And sometimes, yes, sometimes that means pain."

"I hear you." Sienna nodded. "So it's kinda a big deal, no? You signing on to open up for Millionaire Mal on the tour next week? How's it feel to replace Sike-it?"

"Yo . . . I got mad respect for Sike-it, you know? And it's too bad it didn't work out for him, you know? But me and Sike—none of us—we wouldn't even be in this game if Mal didn't pave through for us. Me and my homie, Sir Gee? We just gon' be happy to be there."

"Well," she said, "welcome to Philly. You know this is Mal's hometown, right?"

"Yo . . . that'd be like not knowing Michael Jackson was from Gary, ya dig."

We all laughed.

Piper put his fist in the air, paused for a moment of silence and then said, "Yo . . . Peace to Mike."

"Always," Sienna Jax agreed. "Now, you're in town tonight for Mal's party tonight, right?"

"For sure. Just passin' through before the big show tomorrow night in New York. Had to come and holler at my Philly fam—"

"All of *Philly* is headed to New York, tomorrow." She laughed. "The big tribute to Jam-Master Jay, right? The Apollo."

"Oh, for sure," Piper said. "Yo . . . If there was never no Run-DMC there would be no Piper MC, ya dig?"

I glanced out the window at the rooftop across from us, at all the graffiti on sides of buildings, the wires on rooftops. I was all the way in Philadelphia, Pennsylvania, and I was in a radio station with Piper MC. Yeah, I was still irked at Raq for spending last night with him, but let's keep it real, I'd never had much of a chance anyway. And I didn't know what to make of her stolen credit cards and stolen money, but at least Raq had gotten me here, to this moment in my life. And that was worth a lot. I reached out and squeezed her hand, and she squeezed mine back.

"Some people consider Mal's music more for the party scene these days," Sienna said. "How will you fit in with that vibe?"

"Yo . . . Let me say this . . . Here's what I say . . ."

"And what's that?" Sienna tilted her head and offered a playful smile. "What does Piper think?"

"Yo . . . People say I rap about pain. But there's more if you wanna hear it and listen. . . ." He turned and looked at me. And then he turned back to the microphone.

Sienna nodded. "Right, right . . ."

"Yo . . . Um, *music . . .*" Piper laughed. He went in close to the microphone again, then he played with his keys some more. "For real. I got a treat for y'all coming up real soon. There's always another side to Piper."

Sienna said, "What side is that?"

"Yo . . ." he said, taking time to find the words as he so artfully does, "I got this joint called 'Liar, Liar' that's just so dope. Ladies, y'all out there watchin' these movies, reading these books, thinkin' love is gonna happen so uneventfully. When in fact, it's really the opposite. Love is full with tests. I'm a man, I'm tellin' you. . . . You gotta be willin' to accept something with us. Without cooperation from your mind first, your heart will simply be broken. 'Liar, Liar'—"

Sienna glanced back down at her notes. "That's the upcoming joint with Buckstarr, the chick from the reality show, right?"

"Yo"—he got close to the microphone again—"Buckstarr is on the track, yes. Her and both of her friends, *Boom-boom* and *Vroom-vroom*."

Sienna laughed.

Raq rolled her eyes and then twisted her lips.

"Piper MC," Sienna said, "while you're throwin' all this caution to the ladies . . . For all of 'em listenin', you single?"

"Very," Piper said.

"Well, all right," Sienna said, wrapping up the interview. "Any final words?"

"Yo," Piper said, "life is *good.* I'm backed by the soon-to-be most influential man in the industry—shot out to Mun—and I got my homie Sir Gee riding shotgun. Papers stackin'. Got my mind right." He shifted in his seat and side-eyed Raq. *"Got my hoes . . ."*

Sienna's smile faded. And so did Raq's.

Gee just looked out the window, as if trying not to hear.

I tried to swallow that awkward moment as if it hadn't even happened.

But it had.

"All right, Piper," Sienna said, her voice unaffected but her face definitely a little tense. "Anybody else you wanna get a shout-out to before we let you go get ready for the party tonight?"

"Big up to the Motor, mad love to Philly."

"What do you have to say to those still debating on coming out to Mal's party tonight?"

"I. Will. Be. There." Piper enunciated every word. "And I want to meet all of Philly's finest."

Raq and I darted a look at each other. Without saying it, I could tell that we were both wondering the same thing. *Were we going, too?*

"And yo . . ." Piper leaned in close to the microphone again. "Shout out to Cyn 21. Mad respect. Get better soon, homie."

Sienna signed off, Piper autographed the station's banner in the lobby, and we left the station. Despite what he had said about being single, and about his so-called hoes, Raq still slipped her hand in Piper's as we walked.

Gee walked behind Piper and next to me but put his hands in his pockets. "Good interview, Pipe," he said.

Piper put his free fist to the air, "Appreciate that," he said, exchanging dap with Gee.

"But, um," Raq said, "so who are your *hoes*?"

Piper laughed. "Relax, girl. Y'all know I didn't mean that. First rule in this game, no matter what kinda message you tryna bring? Gotta throw a cuss word, a ho or a bitch line in there, too. Got the intellectuals, yeah, but you got so many more average cats out there than anything. Gotta make sure they hear me, too. Feel me?''

''Whatever, dude,'' was Raq's quick reply, which made Piper and Gee both laugh.

''So about that party tonight?'' Raq asked. ''Me and Glitz are coming, too, right?''

Piper nudged Gee. ''Yo . . . shorty's feisty, huh? Picture me telling her no.''

Gee laughed. ''Yeah. Picture that. . . .''

And it was clear to me then that we *all* knew; what Raq wanted, Raq got.

16

The party that night was at Club Mocha, a trendy two-story club in downtown Philly. THE OFFICIAL HIP IN HIP-HOP, the marquee read. I wore one of the dresses that Raq had bought me, the turquoise one that shimmered when I walked. Hers was hot pink satin and off the shoulder. We ushered in the night with Piper and Gee on velvet couches in the upstairs VIP lounge.

The closest I'd ever come to being inside a club was Jewel's basement at her sixteenth birthday party. Her parents had it decorated for its theme, "Mardi Gras in August," and there were strobe lights and even a disco ball in the center of the room. We had sparkling punch, a deejay (actually just Jewel's cousin Bob), and plenty of dancing. But it was nothing like this!

The VIP lounge had a view of the rest of the club; the four of us were overlooking the crowd of club-dressed hip-hop heads. The music was on point and the scene was bananas. Wall to wall people feeling fine and looking good. In comparison to the

VFW, this crowd was a bit older. There was plenty of dancing, of course, but no ripples of screams and not a lot of laughter. If hip-hop was religion to us, it was just mildly serious to these people, or at least that's how they wanted to appear. Too cool to be crunk. Piper popped a bottle of champagne. Raq laughed when he did, though the sound was so loud it scared me at first.

"Cheers." Raq was raising a glass after Piper had filled it.

Piper filled mine, too, and I raised it. "Cheers back atcha," I said.

The bubbly tasted like bitter ginger ale as it forced heat into my chest. I couldn't help but scowl, but I played it off by grooving to the music. A moment later everything inside of me felt smooth again. Maybe even a tad *smoother.*

A bunch of groupies were at the rope adjacent to our area, patiently awaiting Millionaire Mal's arrival, and a couple of them even looking desperate for Piper's attention. Raq was sitting next to him on the couch, her palm resting on his back as he poured more champagne into her glass.

He put his glass in the air. "Yo . . . To hip-hop . . ."

We all clinked glasses and sipped some more, the taste more pleasing in my chest this time.

Gee reached over and poured more into my glass.

I sat down next to him, hoping he wasn't still sore at me. But even if he was, I knew I had done the right thing last night. No way was I giving up my virginity for Raq's left-over guy.

A song came on, a definite down-South party hopper, and Raq got up to dance. Right in front of Piper—not caring if he got up, too—she kicked it *for* him. And so he stayed sitting, visibly loving every moment of seeing Raq's body gyrate.

Raq turned back to me and yelled, "Must really suck not being us, right, *chica*?"

I raised my glass again. "Hear, hear . . ." Then I downed what was left.

Gee closed his eyes and started rubbing his temples.

"Hey." I nudged him. "You all right?" I couldn't help but wonder if he was tired, had a headache, or just couldn't stand seeing Raq all over Piper when he had tried to get her first.

Gee's eyes popped open and he nodded. "Yeah, I'm good," he said, pouring more champagne into his own glass this time.

I sipped and he immediately poured more in my glass.

He put his hand on my thigh. I felt my neck tighten, and then my stomach.

High-pitched screams filled the room and I jumped free from Gee's touch. We all scrambled to look down at the crowd. Millionaire Mal had arrived on the scene!

Dressed in his signature suit with bright-green dollar signs, Mal was throwing out money as he and his entourage pushed through the crowd. People were diving for paper, snatching ends from one another, just going crazy. Funny. *Now* they were crunk.

Look at him, I thought to myself. *Just making it rain*. . . .

Gee let out a chuckle, "That man is a fool," he said, his voice extra firm as he reached for my hand.

I let him hold it, but became obsessed with ideas on how to pull it back. I could pretend I needed something from my purse. I could pretend I had to scratch my back. . . .

A hush. More stillness. And then I followed Gee's gaze.

From the corner of his eye, he was watching Raq. . .

. . . who was kissing on Piper, who was watching Mal's entrance.

I let my hand fall down into my own lap, took another sip from my glass, and kept watching the crowd. That was easy.

But still, a moment later, I felt Gee's mouth on the side of my neck, and I tensed.

He offered a deep whisper, "This area is about to get real tight and crowded. Let's go out to the truck. . . ."

When I didn't answer, he eventually settled on watching the crowd over the ledge.

I downed what was left in my glass.

A security guy popped his head into the lounge and called out, "Piper . . . you down? Photos with Mal?"

Piper pulled himself from Raq's embrace and security ushered him and Gee off to snap photos with Millionaire Mal.

Now it was just me and Raq up in VIP.

And my glass was empty.

Great.

"Cool party," she said.

"It's definitely what's up," I replied.

She stood up to get a better look over the railing, running her fingers across the gold bar. "Look at all these people, *chica* . . . All here to get a glimpse of Piper. . . ."

"I know," I said.

"Look at 'em. Street CEOs. Straight ballers representin'. If we didn't have these fools with us, we could probably go snatch us one." She turned to me and laughed.

I forced a chuckle. Was Raq saying she didn't even really like Piper?

"I don't know," I said. "Why snatch one of them when you have Piper?"

She rolled her eyes but she didn't answer. "Saw you over there with Gee. You caught up?"

"Gee?" I shot back. "I don't think so. He's cool and everything, but . . ."

Raq dismissed it all with a hand wave. "So forget Gee, then. Who you got?"

I spotted a guy with a shaved head wearing an expensive-looking suit. "Him," I playfully decided.

"All right," she said. "He's too stiff for me. You can have him. . . ."

Laughing, I looked around some more.

"Him." I nodded at a guy who'd just walked through the door. He was tall, real tall, and nice-guy cute.

"Ooh, *chica*," she said, "now, *he* looks like a superstar. Go girl. . . ." She raised her glass in the air and waited for me to toast.

"What are we toasting to?" I yelled over the new music as a louder club song kicked in, something I hadn't heard before.

Raq scrunched up her face and got into the beat of the hype song. "Yo, that's tight," she said, sounding a little like Piper when she did. "To the clubs bangin' it in Philly."

We clinked and sipped. This is what I'd been missing. Me and Raq. Like the good times. When I trusted her.

Finally, I got the nerve and asked her, "So what's really up with you and Piper?"

She actually looked happy that I'd inquired. *"Chica,"* she leaned in and whispered, "let you in on a little secret, all right?"

I braced my heart and put my ear in closer to listen. "Okay . . ."

"I've had better," she said.

Confused, I replied, "Better what?"

She nudged me. *"Chica . . ."*

"What?" I was totally confused.

"Put it like this"—she looked around to make sure they hadn't come up behind us, took a sip, and said—"even my *first time* was better. And you know how horrible that is." She cracked up.

My heart tanked.

Her first time?

She'd told me that she was a virgin, just like I was.

My smile completely fading, I said, "No, Raq. I don't know."

"*Mira,* back in the day when—" She caught herself.

I rolled my eyes and looked away. She'd lied to everyone in the world. I don't know why I ever thought she'd be honest with me. I went over and sat down on the couch, watching as Raq just stood there moving to the music, acting like she hadn't just gotten busted in one of the first lies she'd ever told her so-called best friend. I had honestly believed that this was something she and I had in common. What *hadn't* she lied about?

Piper and Gee came back to the VIP lounge a little while later with a tall guy with sunkissed chestnut skin and a wavy ponytail. They introduced him as the photographer who'd been taking pictures of them with Mal. Now Piper, Gee, and the photographer were over by the ledge, talking with Raq, nodding and laughing, having a good old time.

Whatever. Let 'em talk.

Later, when we all passed through the crowd to leave the club, I remember stopping and picking up a crisp hundred-dollar bill that someone had apparently missed. I couldn't believe my luck. But it made me laugh out loud, like real loud and hearty, when I saw Millionaire Mal's face where Ben Franklin's should've been. I flashed it in front of Piper's face and he immediately twisted his mouth.

"Yo . . . now that's just corny," he said.

So is being a liar, I thought to myself as I glanced over at Raq.

Even worse, though, is being a friend to one.

⬚ ◼ ⬚

We were headed to a private house party in West Oak Lane, or WOL, as Gee said the locals called it: a tree-lined neighborhood in North Philly where the houses were all the same style—two stories with well-manicured lawns—but occasionally different in color. Mostly, they were brick and white, though. This was where the photographer lived.

The house was packed when we got there. Even with a party going on, not a thing looked out of place. The décor was simple and meticulous, and the girls all looked like wannabe fashion models with curious expressions on their faces. *Who are these new people on the scene?* they looked to be wondering. *And are they any competition for me?* I suddenly felt overdressed in all my shimmer. Most of them were in classic black.

"Right over there . . ." I heard someone tell Gee, pointing to a door leading to a patio out back.

At the doorway we were greeted by two men, both of whom

were hesitant to let us onto the porch, which was lit by what seemed to be a hundred tiny tea lights. Gee explained who we were, and they stared too hard into all of our eyes before finally letting us past.

As soon as we stepped out onto the deck, large enough to hold a party itself, I felt like going back inside. There were heat lamps all around, sure, but something was cold about the mood out there. No one was really talking. And everyone seemed to be watching. A waitress in a tiny white dress with a tuxedo cummerbund was walking around with a silver platter of shrimp and cocktail sauce aplenty. Man. I'd never seen something like that at a house party before. The ones I'd gone to, usually after a football game, generally consisted of laughing, dancing, shooting darts, and eating Gino's pizza.

Piper and Gee eyed the host of the party, the photographer, who was sitting at a table near the ledge with a couple of sleazy-looking guys. Another waitress offered us her tray, filled with flutes of champagne.

"No, thanks," I said. I'd had enough at the club.

Raq, however, took a glass and immediately began downing it. "Be right back, *chica*," she told me as she followed Piper and Gee over to the table where the photographer was sitting. And then, not knowing what else to do, I found an empty platinum stool and round table in the corner and sat down.

A woman's voice said, "Hey, sugar? You all right?"

She came up from behind me and took the other seat at the table. She looked like a hooker with all that makeup on her face and wearing a too-tight dress, but still, amid the flow of stuck-up strangers—and considering that Raq had dipped on me—this woman's greeting was welcome. She extended her hand, her long fire-red fingernails..

"Chocolate," she said. She didn't have a tray so I knew she wasn't offering me any.

"That's your name?" I asked.

"On my birth certificate, too." She laughed, too loud to be serious. "You work around here?"

I shook my head no. I didn't even have a job. Never had.

She took a sip of her drink and eyed me. "How do you know Johnny?"

I shrugged. Who was Johnny?

Chocolate laughed again, but eyed me. "If I didn't know any better, I'd think you were a little girl. A teenager or something. . . . You don't even know who Johnny is, do you?"

Piper, Gee, and Raq were sitting with the photographer now and the other guys were up mingling.

"Of course I do," I lied. "The photographer."

Her expression told me I was right.

Then, convincingly (I hoped), I asked, "So how long have *you* known Johnny?"

She said, "Honey, hush. How old I look to you?"

I studied the cracked makeup framing her eyes—wrinkles from stress, I guessed—and factored in the wig she was wearing—probably covering gray—and said, "Hmm, maybe forty, forty-two at the most."

She clasped her hands together, her brass bangles clinking, "Heee . . ." She leaned in. "Just turned fifty-six. Thank you, sugar."

"You're welcome." I smiled at how pleased she was by my accidental compliment.

"You here to model?" she wanted to know.

I felt my face scrunch up. "Yeah right. *No.*" As if anyone would ever pay me to take my picture.

She smiled. "What about your friend?"

"I don't think so," I said. "She sings."

"Ah . . ." She looked over at Raq knowingly. "I see. Well, I met Johnny when he was seventeen years old, making eight dollars an hour bussing tables at the diner near my job. Part-time, at that. Poor thing. He was always stressed, depressed, and carrying on when I went in there for lunch. I introduced him to my friend DaddyMan. That's how Johnny got started taking pictures, you know."

I swallowed. DaddyMan. What kind of guy is named *DaddyMan*?

"Next I know, he's blowing *up.* Wanted to know if I was tired of working the corner and how long did I plan to *keep* doing it. I said, 'Till something better comes along. . . .' His business was boomin' by then. I've been his eyes and ears ever since."

I looked over at the table where Raq was sitting.

What kind of photographer hires a prostitute to help with his business?

And I listened some more.

She said, "All these years later, here I am. He's like a son to me, now."

She seemed so cool that I felt I could be honest. "Chocolate?" I said.

"Yeah, sugar?"

"Just keepin' it real, I actually don't know Johnny. I'm just here with my friends."

She smiled a bit more. "Uh-*huh*."

Looking over at Raq, at Gee, at Piper, and thinking about home, so far away, I sensed the heat of tears on my face. I was sitting there with Chocolate, yet I had never felt so totally alone. "I'm not even from here," I said, my voice quivering a bit.

She gave me a napkin that was wrapped around her glass, "Here you go, sugar. . . ."

"Sorry," I said, dabbing my eyes dry. "I'm just tired. It's been a long day. It's been a long . . ." I shook my head and wiped away my tears.

She nodded her understanding. And this time when she spoke, I noticed her teeth were stained with lipstick. "Young girls nowadays, y'all got soooo many options," she said. "Wasn't so easy in my day."

I sniffed. "What do you mean?"

She looked over at Raq. "Your friend"—she nodded—"she wanna be a model?"

"A model? No. I told you, she's a singer."

"Well she's over there with a phot-tog-gra-*pher*, sugar. She must want to do some posing for him." Chocolate sighed. "Now, I know Johnny—been knowing him for years—and nobody comes to his house unless they wanna deal with Johnny. He's a businessman."

"What are you talking about?" I asked. Then I gestured to Raq again. "We met him at a club earlier, he took pictures of my friends with Millionaire Mal. We're just here for the after-party."

She looked sympathetic, but in a way that seemed kind of phony to me. She all but said what it looked like she was thinking: *Poor baby. You're so stupid.*

I said, "Raq's trying to be a singer, really. She's good, too."

"She got a demo?"

"No. Not yet. . . ."

Chocolate looked at me, her long, fake eyelashes too distracting for me to be comfortable looking directly back at her.

"You ain't nothin' but a baby," she said.

"Whatever," I said. "I'm not a kid."

Then she added, "Look, I'm in the position—thanks to Johnny—where I don't have to see dollar signs for every young pretty girl I meet. Twenty years ago I'd have introduced you to a whole 'nother world, sugar. I worked the streets for a long time, helpin' young girls just like yourself get on their feet, learn the hustle." She leaned in closer. "I know a runaway when I see one, okay? So quit the bullshit. I can smell it. And the fear."

Runaway. The word hit me like a burst of cold air, and I almost shivered.

"Johnny, on the other hand?" she said. "He ain't nice as me. Man had to learn to fly with no wind for his wings. Born into a slum life. Had to rise up, do the best he could. He's a good guy, don't get me wrong. I love 'im. But he spares no one. Guess he figures he had to look down the barrel of desperate times and do desperate things, so others should, too. He's no joke, sugar. A *hawk*."

I looked over at Johnny. Just then he was taking his hand to his hair, his fingers stroking his ponytail as he leaned back and chatted away.

"Your friend? I know her type. So much defiance in her eyes. . . . They fall the hardest sometimes. Either that or they make it the furthest. I was just like her, I'm tellin' you. Looks. Sass. Oh, Johnny's over there loving her right now, trust me. She'll do what she gotta do to survive. But you . . ." Chocolate looked at me and smiled. I shrugged. "What? I said I don't want to be a model."

She laughed. "I know. And your friend, if she's smart, she'll walk away, tell him no thank you, find another way to support that little career of hers she wants, but look at her . . . you see she's still sitting over there."

"What's the big deal about modeling?" I asked.

"*This* kind of modeling?" She laughed. "Oh, sugar. It's a big deal all right," she said. "I don't know where you're from, but trust me, *you don't want to be here*. Take yourself on home."

I was shaken by a creepy feeling.

Raq would do anything for her dreams, I knew, but *anything*? Really?

From the first time I met her, from the time she was born, probably, Raq had talked of one thing and one thing only. Fame. Tonight, she was willing to take what I guess she believed would be a giant leap in that direction.

From across the room, we finally locked into eye contact.

She was smiling. Triumphant.

17

It was two o'clock in the morning and we were sitting in Johnny's basement office. Nasty-looking nude photography was hanging on the wood-paneled walls like family photos would in a sane person's home. While Piper and Gee were still upstairs, mixing with the rest of the after-party crowd, the king of this wicked jungle—Johnny—sat across from me and Raq as she signed paper after paper rescinding what was left of her innocence.

"Are you crazy?" I had whispered on our way down the steps.

"Uh. Not," she had quipped. "Do you know how lucky I am? Everyone's gonna know my name."

A frazzled looking model Johnny had introduced as his assistant peeked in.

She said, "Something to drink? Soda? Tea?"

"I'll take a tea," Raq said. I'd have asked for the same if I thought I wouldn't hurl after a sip of anything hit my stomach. I was so disgusted.

Up close, Johnny was handsome. His eyes, though, seemed dark and shifty, and they never met with mine.

After Raq finished signing the papers, he got up from his desk.

"Be right back," he said before leaving the room.

The assistant returned with a mug of hot water and a tea bag.

"Thanks," Raq said as casually as if we were in a café back home.

Raq blew onto her brewing tea. "I was just thinking about my first song," she said. "We should probably do something up-tempo, you know? Like with a crazy snare drum. A club banger. Follow that up with a ballad . . ."

"Okay, so just never mind the trifling mistake you're about to make? Let's ignore all that and just talk about a song you *might* get to record someday? Raq!" I wanted to shake her. I wanted to scream.

She nudged me, her voice more mellow than usual. "*Chica* . . . I'm the one who should be nervous. Do you know how famous I'm getting ready to be?"

I rolled my eyes. "Are you serious?"

"My first photo shoot . . ." she said, looking around the office in awe. "Everyone does a photo shoot like this when they're just starting off."

"No. They don't," I said. And I really didn't even care if she got mad. She didn't, though. Not at all.

"You've got so much to learn," she said matter-of-factly. "About life. About the industry. *Mira.* No matter how hot you are vocally, they really don't care 'less you're at boiling point in the looks. If men wanna see you on the page, wanna download you on the Net, shoot, that's buzz. Plus, we're from Toledo? Please. I gotta come with it hard. This is gonna be a good move for me, *chica*. Trust. And be happy."

I faked a smile. "Cheers!"

She said, "Look, I know I got talent. But break down the book value for me if nobody knows who I am, *chica*."

"Right . . ." I sighed. "Gotcha." Apparently I just wasn't going to get through to her no matter what I said.

"There comes a time in life when you're gonna have to grow up, *chica*. You're gonna have to learn that being an adult means doing grown-up things."

Yeah, right. Lying so much had Raq believing that we were actually adults.

"Look," she said, pointing to a picture on the wall. Up there was Buckstarr sitting naked on the hood of a sports car.

"So what if she *is* famous?" I snapped back. "She slutted herself on reality television and porn magazines to do it. Is it really worth it?"

Raq laughed an annoying laugh. "Oh, *chica . . .*"

I made a ticking sound with my tongue and rolled my eyes.

Johnny returned and I could've hacked back and spit at his face. His smile was wicked. "Are you ready, Raquel?"

"Born ready." She placed her mug on the desk and grabbed her bag, a quilted purple trendy clutch she'd bought at the King of Prussia Mall, and made her exit.

My heart was beating harder than I'd ever felt it, even up to my ears, and my neck seemed paralyzed in tension. What do you do when the person you want to rescue willingly walks *into* the fire? What if she doesn't even flinch at the heat, but says "Back in a few, *chica*" instead?

In the next room, I could hear Johnny talking to Raq through the paneling. I guessed it must have been his photo studio.

Are you ready, Raquel?

"She goes by Raq," I wished I had said.

But then again, maybe I didn't even know what she wanted to be called anymore, or who she was.

I wondered if I'd ever really known.

⌗ ◪ ⌗

First Gee had eyes for my best friend.

Then he'd helped her put her body, her soul actually, up for sale.

How could he continue to pretend that he was digging me, too?

And how could I continue to act like the sight of him didn't repulse me?

Gee's mouth on my neck again was making me nauseous.

It was late Wednesday—or really, early Thursday morning— our last night in Philadelphia. We were back at the hotel after Raq's "photo shoot." I should have been hyped. Tomorrow was the Jam-Master Jay tribute at the Apollo and I was finally going to see New York City, but it was hard to feel happy after all that had happened. On top of that, I was lying in a hotel room and Gee was stuck with me, the overflow.

I didn't know why he was trying so hard to act like he was digging me.

Or why I didn't punch him when he nonchalantly crawled into bed next to me.

He said, "What's up with you?" I took a deep breath and really tried to sound cheerful. "Nothing. Nothing at all. I'm good. . . ." I scooted away from him. And then over some more.

Poor Gee. Thought he was a hustler. Whole time he'd been got. He believed the lie about Hitz from the beginning. Ha! For all we knew, Hitz might have never even swatted a fly in his life, let alone hit a woman. Hitz never even knew Raq's name.

Gee took off his white T-shirt and crisp denim jeans,

meticulously placing his blinged-out belt buckle on the nightstand. My heart completely froze.

What was he getting ready to do? Oh, God. But he just lay there in his boxer briefs and platinum rope chain. His body was solid, not at all flabby, like a middleweight boxer's, and for the first time, I noticed the tattoo on his left arm. In Old English lettering, it read, PRESSURE.

Part of me wanted to explain to him what was really going on in my head, but I wasn't sure he'd understand. How I wanted to be in the arms of a guy who was really digging me, not one who just kissed down my neck when it was convenient for him, when the girl he actually wanted was distracted. Mentally, I was already heading home. Physically, though, I was still on the road. In a room with Gee.

He said, "You just layin' over there starin' at me. Like something's wrong. . . ."

It is. I don't belong here.

And I never really did.

But I sat up. And I looked at him, straight-on. "Just tell me. Whose idea was it?" I asked. "The photo shoot?"

"Oh, my goodness," he said. "Is that why you're over there on mute?" he joked. "Because Raq got buck?"

I grimaced at hearing the reality of it. But then I nodded. "Yeah."

He said, "Look, it was her idea. We just made the introduction."

"Oh," I said. Even if that was true, it didn't make me feel better about what had happened.

"What?" he joked. "You her personal guardian now? The moral police?"

"No." I frowned. But then I thought about it. "But . . . I am her friend."

"Look. She's a grown woman," he said. Then he got up and went to the other bed. "Turn the light off when you get done with your moral patrolling." He yanked back the covers and looked determined to just get some sleep.

I glanced out the window, noticing the thump of a hip-hop beat coming from next door. Piper and Raq. I said to Gee, "It's not that I don't think you're cool, Gee. . . ."

"Can't tell. . . ." He pulled a pillow over his head, drowning out the music.

I got up, went over to his bed, and crawled in beside him. I understood what he was feeling. Rejection is a rough thing. For whatever reason, I reached in and wrapped my arms around Gee, pulling the pillow off of his face. He let me. But didn't move otherwise.

He said, "We should probably leave out for New York about noon. It's about a two-hour drive. When we get into the city, we can swing down to Times Square, maybe unload a few more CDs."

"Can you see the Empire State Building from there?" I asked.

"The Empire State Building?" he said. "Are you serious? You can see it from everywhere in New York."

I felt myself smiling inside as I touched his arm. Traced the letters. Ink over a big solid muscle. "Nice tat," I said. "Pressure, huh?"

"Without it, we wouldn't have the most beautiful gem in the world," he said through a yawn.

"Diamonds," I said.

"Oh yeah." He sounded impressed. "You know about that, huh?"

"One of my old friends back home, she comes from a family of jewelers. Jones Diamonds. They even named her Jewel." I thought back to the time when Jewel had taken me on a tour of a back room of one of their stores and one of the gem setters had explained to us how diamonds are made. He reminded me of a librarian, excited about helping me find a book on a shelf, when I'd asked where diamonds come from.

"Diamonds," he'd told me, taking special care as he placed one on a white cloth, *"are formed under tremendous heat and pressure. These extreme conditions only exist beneath the earth's surface, where temperatures can reach thirteen hundred degrees. Atoms ultimately form into crystals and the crystals eventually make their way to the earth's surface through pipes*

and channels. *The pipes or channels contain volcano magma,* *which rises with the diamonds and deposits them on the earth's* *surface. That's when we find them."* His voice was a cautious whisper as he let us take turns holding it. He added. *"It all* *starts with heat. And pressure."*

"Know how to tell a real diamond from a fake one?" Gee asked me.

I smiled. That had been part of the jewelry lesson as well. "By its shine," I said. "If it's been cut correctly, a real diamond reflects light on all sides. A fake one doesn't."

Gee nodded.

The music next door shifted to another song and seemed to grow even louder.

PRESSURE. Must be an everyday reminder, I thought as I looked at his arm, tracing my fingers along each letter again. Maybe when Gee looked in the mirror—stressed about all the weight Mun-E was always putting on his and Piper's shoulders—that's what Gee uses to remind himself of what all the pressure can eventually produce.

18

The skyline of New York City was like a scene from a Batman movie. It looked like Gotham for real! Smoky and dark. Huge. So ugly and mean and yet so impossibly beautiful and alluring. I wanted to take a giant can of spray paint and spell out the words GLITZ WAS HERE right across it all. I had never seen so many high buildings! And they were all so cluttered and hemmed up next to each other. Endless dreams and endless possibilities. And so many determined people! Even the old lady crossing the street pushing her fold-up shopping cart looked to be on a mission.

Okay, I said to myself, my face pressed against the cold window as we swerved and jerked along in traffic, *where is it*?

And no sooner than I'd thought it, I heard myself gasp. There it was.

It reminded me of a tall stack of gray LEGOs with a tall steeple atop. I took a deep breath. Right underneath what looked to be an antenna was an illuminated section of New York City's tallest building and I knew that that was it. The eighty-sixth floor. Where he proposed. Where she said yes. My parents . . .

I felt Raq tugging at my arm. "We're here, *chica*! We made it!"

A hot tear stalled in the corner of my eye, and yet a smile crept across my face. Yes. I had definitely made it.

They were up there once.

Happy. Smiling. Laughing. So in love.

Their whole lives ahead of them . . .

And then, when I couldn't look any longer, I closed my eyes.

By the time I had opened them again, Gee had made a turn. Now we were facing a sea of tall apartment buildings. Gee was whipping through the potholed streets so fast that it was hard for me to turn around at first. Still, I craned my head the best that I could.

But my view of the Empire State Building was gone.

Just like my parents.

⌗ ⬥ ⌗

Harlem. You could hear the mouthwatering thud of bass coming from the theater as we pulled up at the Apollo that night. The vertical marquee was yellow with red letters, just like on television. It had been hard to get ready in the Hummer, but I felt amazing in my black satin minidress, knock-off pearls, and faux fur shawl. I glanced over at Raq, who looked ready for a performance at the Grammys. Her makeup was worthy of a magazine cover, flawless, and her getup—a sequined halter jumpsuit—was incredible. I couldn't help but be happy for her, despite what she'd done last night. In her own way she'd made it, even if—in my eyes—she'd compromised too much to do so. After this, her performance with Piper, who knew how things were going to blow up for her!

Pimped-out cars and SUVs swooped in and out of the security-protected car line, drivers hell-bent on showcasing the arrival of their hot-fashioned rappers who'd come to help honor the late and incomparably great Jam-Master Jay.

When Sir Gee hit the brakes and the Hummer screeched to a halt, I literally had to remember to breathe. I turned around and sucked in the skyline once again. We were really in New York City! Sir Gee showed the guard his ID, signed a paper, and parked in one of the coned-off spacesbehind the building. .

Piper rubbed his hands before getting out. "Yo . . . " he said. "Let me at 'em."

Tugging down my minidress so it wouldn't ride up when I got out of the truck, I pushed back my shoulders and gave my head a quick feel, making sure that my hair was tidy in its bun, smooth and classic according to Raq. With my head held high and a confident face securely fastened on, I looked over at Raq for a quick check. She reached in and—with her fingertip— made sure my berry-colored lipstick was just right.

She shot a confused look at me. "You have on eyeliner?"

I shrugged. "Special days call for special things," I said. "I can't believe you just noticed. I borrowed yours."

She pressed her finger on my arm. "Hot, *chica!*" she said, then made a fizzing sound.

"You're the one. Rock the mic tonight," I reminded her.

And I knew she would. Raq had been practicing with Piper in the car for the last hour. Raquel Marissa Diaz was more than ready for that stage.

Together, the four of us headed toward the back entrance.

A guy wearing earphones and holding a clipboard approached us in a hurry. "You're on in about forty-five minutes," he said, giving Piper and Sir Gee some dap before taking the track for the deejay from Sir Gee. "Welcome to Harlem."

Piper stopped then, double-kissed two of his fingers, and then double knocked his fist to his chest. He nodded and allowed a solemn expression to form on his face. "Yo . . . appreciate that."

Sir Gee added, "Thanks, man."

Backstage was congested and confusing. Too many people and not enough room. Unlike the show at the VFW in Ohio, there weren't any random groupies or people with passes, though. The only people who were backstage were either working or getting ready to perform.

Immediately, I recognized faces.

Nelly. The Beastie Boys. Young Joc. Damon Dash. Trick Daddy. Oh my goodness! MC Lyte. And Lil' Kim!

Everyone who was anyone in hip-hop was there. There were the bigwigs and all the eager-to-be-next up-and-comers like Piper and Sir Gee. A man with platinum grills and a floppy fur coat rushed past us, drenched in sweat from having just performed, and instantly I recognized him. Sike-it MC. He gave man hugs to Piper and Sir Gee, the MCs taking over his position on Mal's tour, before pressing on with his crew.

"Hey, *chica*." Raq turned to me and smiled.

I shrugged and gave her a smile right back. "You're gonna kill it," I told her.

And then we go home.

Neither Raq nor I—and not even Piper or Sir Gee—was born yet in the 1970s, when rap music crept into the souls of African and Latin Americans, inching up the walls of every club, basement, and bedroom radio in the Bronx, caressing ears and changing lives forever. Decades ago DJ Kool Herc, Lovebug Starski, Keith Cowboy, DJ Hollywood, the Sugarhill Gang, and Afrika Bambaataa labored into birth a complete new lifestyle called hip-hop, and look at us now—me and Raq, Piper and Sir Gee—backstage in Harlem, one borough away from the Bronx, where it'd all begun. I wasn't alive yet when it all happened, but boy was I glad that it had.

Hip-hop.

Highly. Intelligent. People.

Helping. Other. People.

The paparazzi's eyes were on us as we made our way through the crowd. Raq was treading enviable water, and of all the chicks lined up and appearing primed to sing hook, she was the prettiest, no doubt.

And I knew once she was out on that stage, she was going to make it impossible for anyone in the house to do anything but clap.

The backstage coordinator led us to the wings. "Meet here in exactly thirty minutes. Until then, your seats are in row five if you want to sit in on the show." He handed each of us our passes. Our own—*ahem*—VIP passes.

Raq winked at me. *"Chica . . ."*

Piper said, "Yo . . . Y'all go on and enjoy the show. Meet y'all back here." Raq and I both squealed. And hurried off.

⋈

The blue-toned illumination on the stage was beautiful against the wood, and the sudden absence of any house lights signified the beginning of the next act. The very stage where the Jackson Five had performed. Ella Fitzgerald. Billie Holiday. James Brown. The Isley Brothers. Luther Vandross. Fat Joe. Lauryn Hill. Even though I was sure Gramma was ready to kill me, I had to believe a small part of her would be excited that I was here, where so many of her own idols had performed.

Everyone clapped and cheered as Bow Wow appeared onstage. We were in the fifth row center, so close I felt like I could reach out, stretch my arm a bit, and touch his pant leg.

I glanced over at Raq, her eyes glistening with so much hope.

So much had happened. So much had changed.

But we were here. We were really *here*. And only the two of us knew how much that meant.

Without looking at me, Raq slapped my thigh. "We did it, *chica*."

And then, with her energetic smile, Raq the dreamer, the no-nonsense good-time girl, playfully jerked her head and looked at me. "Let's just kick it, all right?" Her way of apologizing, of wanting to pretend like things were all good again. I wanted the same.

"All right. Cool," I replied. And I turned back around and got comfortable in my seat.

After Bow Wow's hyped performance, time passed in a surrealist slow motion as Arnold Crane, the rickety-looking president of some local youth outreach center that had cosponsored the event, read from a series of note cards. His words pounded in my head like slurred mumbo-jumbo. Line after line after line of boring statistics on the perils of just about anything that kids were facing in America. I had no idea what-all he said, because after a while I just tuned him out. I didn't want to hear about delinquent kids. I was one of them now. But not for long. *Just one more night,* I thought. *Then tomorrow I'll be home.*

A radio station manager, rocking a Hot-97 T-shirt, was next.

Inside, I smiled.

In every city . . .

Always a ninety-something.

He gave a few shot-outs to some of the other event sponsors, pulled a couple of names for door prizes—hair products from Dark and Lovely, a gym membership, and subscriptions to a bunch of hip-hop magazines—and then he introduced some local comedian who was actually pretty funny. He kept the crowd energized until Fat Joe came out.

When he hit the stage, Raq offered me a smooth smile and her signature wink, the one that means *It's all good.* We kicked it so hard while Fat Joe performed, not missing a beat of his set as an opportunity to swing our hips.

Judging from the screams throughout the crowd, they were definitely feeling Fat Joe, too. He was incredible. *Wait,* I thought to myself, *until they hear Piper MC featuring Sir Gee . . . and Raq.*

¤ ✖ ¤

Once we got backstage, Piper briefed Raq. "Me and Gee are gonna work the stage. You just stay posted up off to the right," he said. In other words, it was Piper's show and Raq had to remember to play the background. No fancy tricks.

I got it, and Raq got it, too. "Whatever you say, Pipe," she responded.

"Sounds good," Sir Gee added.

"Yo . . ." Piper bowed his head to pray in silence.

I did the same.

It was showtime. And no one in the house was more hungry for that spotlight than Raq. I was one hundred percent positive that she could handle what sounded like a full house. And I'm sure she would have if she had been able to perform.

It all happened so fast.

"Excuse me," a soft voice said from behind us.

And then, there she stood.

Buckstarr.

And an entourage of cameras filming her.

Guess she brought the reality show reunion with her.

Reaching in to tap Piper on his shoulder, she was tall, fancy, and impossibly stacked in all-pink leather. She had seemed amused by the sight of Raq and me in the recording studio late last Saturday night, but tonight her face looked equipped for war.

I felt like crying out to God to protect us. *Please let us get through this without a fight breaking out.*

Raq caught a glimpse of Buckstarr, saw how smooth and easy Sir Gee and Piper reacted, and I saw a flicker of something cross her face—anger? Disbelief?—before she hid it under a blank expression.

Dreams. The closer you get, the harder the reach.

The harder the reach, the more you want it.

The more you want it, the more you'll do to get it.

Raq looked at Piper. Shook her head. "Don't even play me, Pipe. . . ."

Piper looked at Gee. Gee looked at Buckstarr.

And Buckstarr turned around so she was eye to eye with Raq. They stared each other down until Raq glanced at the camera, filming it all, and looked away.

In that moment, I knew it was set. Raq wasn't going onstage that night. But she wasn't going to fight about it either. She was gonna grin and bear it. And for the first time ever since I'd known her she looked like Raquel to me, not Raq. Not exactly soft, but not hard, either. Human.

Mun-E was right there, too. He looked like a bulldog hungry for a bone. It was like he could taste all the money he was going to make off of Piper and Buckstarr's song and he was licking his chops.

Buckstarr smiled, shrugged, and said to Piper, "You ready?"

On cue, Piper, Sir Gee, and Buckstarr followed the stage-hand out to the wing so they could enter the stage. Had to give it to her, Buckstarr definitely looked like a celebrity.

Buckstarr's performance with Piper and Gee was hot, no denying that. Raq and I watched from backstage. And I learned a big lesson in the cutthroat music business that night. After they sang "Liar, Liar," after the crowd went bananas, an army of soldiers toting big cardboard boxes appeared in the crowd. Buckstarr had had a gazillion silk-screened T-shirts pressed with pictures of Piper, Sir Gee, and her—dressed in a patent-leather bodysuit—on the front. Across the back were the words LIAR, LIAR, PIPER'S NEW SINGLE FEATURING SIR GEE AND BUCKSTARR.

It's not always the best singer who gets the gig. Sometimes it's about the hustle, the person who's most determined to eat. That night, Buckstarr was the one who trumped.

When Buckstarr, Piper, and Sir Gee left the stage, the cameras and screams exploding, Raq and I both knew that "Liar, Liar" had hit the ball all the way back to Fifth Third Field in Toledo, where the Mud Hens played baseball.

But before then, ever so gracefully at the end of his set, Piper had folded his hands together and rested his eyes. With the spotlight upon him, I remember seeing the sweat pouring down his face. His voice echoed from the rafters.

"Yo . . . Y'all gotta follow Piper. I'm gonna be doing major things. . . ."

19

After the show, we were pressing through security, doing our best to keep up with Piper and Gee, trying to get from backstage out to the truck, when a woman wearing a stiff business suit—she looked clearly out of place—hurried out of nowhere, stopped in front of Piper, and got his attention. A serious fan, maybe?

She flashed a badge. "Excuse me," she said. "May I have a moment with you?"

Piper raised an eyebrow and tried to keep stepping. "Who, me? For what?"

She held up a picture and said, "Do you recognize the girl in this photo? Know someone by the name of Ann? Ann Michelle Lewis?"

My heart landed with a thump in my shoes. Raq and I both slowed.

Simultaneously, we backed up and blended in with the crowd. I ducked my face behind Raq and she was careful to keep enough distance between herself and Gee, whose big body was blocking the view of Piper and the lady.

Gee laughed. "Ann Michelle?"

"No ma'am," I heard Piper say. "I've never met anyone named Ann Michelle."

The lady looked at Piper for a couple of seconds and then at Gee.

"Do you," she asked him, "know the whereabouts of a teen-ager named Ann Michelle?"

"A teen—? *Yo* . . . " Gee said. "Um. Lady . . . No thanks."

I couldn't tell if they really didn't recognize me from the photo—it was my class picture from school last year and I was wearing my uniform, looking totally corny—or if they were just covering.

The lady seemed to be saying something else, but I couldn't make out what it was. I peeked over Raq's shoulder. The woman was pressing on through the crowd away from us. Whew. But Raq didn't move yet. So neither did I.

I heard Mun's voice next. He was having words with Gee.

"You wanna tell me what that was all about?"

"Man, how would I know?"

"You wanna tell me why one minute Hitz is bugging me about some Latin girl, then you're calling me, telling me you got some Latin girl you want to sing with Piper, the next minute I got five-oh knocking at my office, sayin' they're lookin' for a Latin girl of interest from Toledo—"

"Man, what?"

"Listen to me," Mun's voice was firm. *"Don't* be a liability. KFC is hiring."

With that, Mun stormed past without giving Gee a chance to respond.

"Chica!" Raq forced me to look at her. "Mun played us—"

She sighed and then she shrugged. "Well, you're the one they want. Not me. Judge and Kitty'll be over me in no time. Your grandmother actually cares. Look how many times she called."

"Kitty called for you, too!"

"And? That's because me running away looks bad for them. Not like they really care."

"She sounded terrified, Raq. I answered your phone the other morning. You were out when I woke up."

"Who cares? And please tell me you didn't fall for her dramatics. She's a judge's wife, a public figure." Raq rolled her eyes. "It's part of her *job* to be phony."

"She sounded panicked. Could have fooled me."

"So what?" she said. "It's different for me. That's not my real blood. My real blood doesn't really care. Why should Kitty matter?"

"I think we should both just give up. Turn ourselves in. We had our fun. We got to meet Piper. We got to come to New York. Piper and Gee are gonna catch heat if we don't. We—"

"Give up?" Raq said with a laugh. "Never," she spat. "I'm not ever going back there."

I said, "Well, then, now what? Because I gotta get home. You promised you'd get me home at the end of all this. Remember?"

"*Chica.*" She put her hands together and pleaded with her eyes. "You're asking me to do all this stuff, you're saying all these things, and I don't know . . ." Her voice sounded so uncertain. "I don't know . . ."

Those were three words I never thought I'd hear her say.

Never before had I known Raq to not have the answer.

Of course I knew, I always knew, that I'd have to go home eventually. This had started as a one-night adventure, and then it had turned into almost a whole week. For a minute there, it had seemed like it might even be forever. But now it was all over.

Poof.

◫ ◪ ◫

Some people live their whole lives chasing after their dreams, going to school, studying hard or working two jobs just to put pretty dresses on their daughters.

Or granddaughters.

Some people stand in lines for hours or even days to

audition—for one single shot—in front of four judges who can decide their fate as singers.

Some people run miles and miles every day, spend hours training and practicing just to be the best they can be at putting balls through hoops or jumping hurdles on tracks.

And some people have all the talent they'll ever need inside of them, but they only know how to steal, cheat, and sacrifice their soul to share it with the world.

Some people will do anything to get famous.

I'd lost track of all the lies Raq told or the number of people she tricked to get ahead in our so-called journey. Including me. I guess Raq never even really had a plan. But she knew where she wanted to go and would do anything—literally—along the way to get us there.

Truth is, I always knew in my heart that there were other ways, that Raq didn't have to rip credit cards or steal money from the two people in her life who had really tried to help her. And now I wondered about the people the credit cards had been stolen *from*. How had they gotten them in the first place? By working hard, I supposed. And that was something I could respect.

When I'd put on that fancy belt or that lace camisole, I hadn't considered the lady who owned it. But I thought about her now. How hard had she worked at her job to make the money to buy those nice things? And how did she feel when she finished her workout at the motel to find her fancy stuff all gone?

I remember standing backstage next to Raq that night after the officer asked Piper about me, closing my eyes and gently pushing my head against the wall where we were standing. And I recall how quiet Raq was.

It seemed like an eternity, until finally I heard her say, "*Chica,* we're gonna be cool. Everything is going to be okay."

I'm sure that if I had opened my mouth to say anything, I would have howled, crying instead. So I just thought to myself, *Okay.*

Piper and Gee were waiting in the truck when we got outside.

Neither of them said a word at first.

The truck was running but the radio wasn't playing.

"Yo . . ." Piper sighed. "Ann Michelle?"

So he *had* recognized me from the picture. Even in my fancy dress and makeup, even with my new name, I was still the same person after all.

Gee asked, "How old are y'all for real?"

"Look," I immediately began, "I just gotta get home. Y'all can drop me on the way back to Detroit and I swear you'll never hear from me again."

Raq said, "*She* needs to get back to Ohio."

"Yo . . . So you was, like, teenagers, the whole time?" Piper raised an eyebrow at me. "When we were talking music and philosophies and . . ." Then at Raq, "Yo . . . When we was . . ."

Gee shook his head. "Wild."

Raq said, "Look, *I'm* not trying to go back to Ohio. I'm—"

The knocks at the window were so loud. All of us jumped.

Four uniformed cops were waiting.

The show was over. Take a bow.

Gee rolled down his window.

"Handcuffs won't be necessary," one of the officers said to us. "As long as you cooperate."

Like a deranged woman, Raq just chuckled. And kept chuckling.

As for me, I started crying, and it felt like I might never stop.

An officer led me out of the Hummer to the police car. And twice my knees buckled as I walked.

Funny. Even though I knew the road back to Ohio was going to be long, I finally felt relief, like eventually things would be lighter again. No more stolen credit cards. No more stolen cash. No more late nights with sleazy photographers. No more running. No more.

I glanced back at the truck, tried to get one last look Piper, but, through my tears, I could only see the blur of his white wristband as he explained things to one of the officers. I never even got one last good look at his face. Gee's either.

But then again, I didn't have to. How could I ever forget them?

¤ ◼ ¤

Raq rolled in a separate patrol car from me, and hers was in front.

I kept watching the back of her head the whole ride back down the turnpike, hoping that she'd turn around and look at me, offer an eye roll, a smile, that wink. But she never looked back. Not even once.

20

"I'm sorry, Gramma," I said in between sniffles, pulling a crinkled-up napkin from my pocket.

Her stare was far scarier than any of her threats had been.

Gramma stood in my bedroom doorway, a fat black belt in hand. "Yes. You. Are. Any child that'd take it upon herself to leave a *good home*—all the children in the world wishing they *had* a warm place to sleep at night—you're so right, you are so sorry!"

Now I was heaving.

"Slobbering and carrying on," she said. "Naw. What's up now? Go 'head witcha bad self. You grown. Be tough. Come on, now, sit up straight! Tell me now what you are and aren't gonna do! Tough enough to be a heavyweight champion, huh? Huh, Ann Michelle Holyfield? Ann Michelle Tyson. You bad. Come on . . . Sending postcards and things. Name is Glitter now, huh?"

She walked the belt closer to me.

I waited until my heaving stopped and said, "I am so sorry, Gramma. I am. Really."

"Left outta here with this bedroom a mess. Clothes strewn all over the floor in the closet."

"I said I'm sorry. So . . ."

She gestured at my desk, a pile of books and a stack of papers waiting neatly. "All the work you've missed from school!" She gripped the belt. "I'd wear your behind out if I didn't think I'd kill you, I am that upset with you, child."

"I'm so sorry . . ." was all I could say. And it was truly how I felt.

She said, "Press a skirt real good tonight, you hear? And that blouse had better be crisp for church in the morning, ya hear me?"

"Yes, Gramma. Okay."

"God's gonna have to help me with this one, otherwise, I'd kill you. Jail is for that little friend of yours, but for you . . ."

She stood before me and raised a hand over my head.

I braced myself, waiting for a slap.

Instead, I felt the light touch of her warm, bony hand on my chin as she lifted my face. My eyelids fell closed, but she gripped my chin tighter until I looked at her again.

Her face was wild with anger.

And yet there was a tear welling in the corner of her eye.

"You listen to *me*." She jerked my face a bit. "What y'all did was bad. And I mean real, real bad. You don't even *know* what my prayers were . . . what I was begging God to spare you from out there. . . ."

She swallowed. "But you're home now. And don't you be ashamed, you hear? You go to school on Monday and you hold your head up. They might look at you strange and maybe even say mean things about you. . . . So be it! You was but a fool. Lord, Lord, Lord, you was a fool. You and me both know that. But that's who God protects best, babies and fools. And we all got to be both at some point in our lives. So you forget telling me you're sorry. Best if you tell God. Ya hear?"

My lip quivering, I nodded.

I felt her fingers let go of my face and watched as she left the room.

I love you, too, Gramma, I thought.

She hadn't said it, but I knew she meant it. And I did, too.

◻ ◼ ◻

Sometimes I like to imagine what it would have been like if the show had gone another way.

I picture me and Raq in the audience again, back out in our seats at the Apollo, rocking and head-nodding to Fat Joe.

Raq's phone starts vibrating. It's Pipe.

"Come backstage?" Raq shouts. "Already? For what?"

After hanging up, she looks over and tells me, "Buckstarr

showed up." Only then she says, "But Piper put her in her place. He said for me to come on and get ready to perform."

Instead of watching from the wings, I imagine that I stay out in the house, fifth row center, and—ten minutes later—Raquel Marissa Diaz walks out onstage with Piper and Gee.

Raq.

She struts out onstage, the princess of hip-hop, all but a tiara.

And when her French-tipped fingernails touch the bright silver microphone, the spotlight catches the mic. I imagine a flash of magic spreading out over the entire place, forcing the audience into hush. They wait.

Piper spits his bars.

And then, she sings.

I have to resist the urge to dab my eyes with pride, throwing my hands in the air and rocking with the rhythm of the song instead.

I imagine Raq's delivery—so heartfelt, so amazing, her raspy voice so sincere, that she owns the stage. And the night. The hook is so incredible that Gee and even Piper, too, soon go unnoticed by the crowd.

Raq used to propose scenarios for the future, how her talent was going to make her a legend, how she was going to grace the cover of every magazine imaginable—not just the ones for Latinas and hip-hop—and how she was going to say in her interviews that she always knew she was going to be a star. And how I was going to be right there with her.

She used to throw her head back and close her eyes, the sun adding heat and shine to her skin, and sit there looking like she was literally picturing everything she talked about.

I can still see it. And I probably always will.

Did I really know her for just over a month? It seemed like so much longer. Like a lifetime, almost.

Sometimes I still don't know what to make of it all.

Sometimes it's fun just to kick back and remember.

Sometimes, if I close my eyes tight, I can even hear us laughing. . . .

Piper. Gee. Raq. And me. Toasting silly things like *fine dining at Burger King.*

It's amazing how impossible it can seem, trying to get famous.

And yet how sometimes it can also happen.

Four months later, I turned on the television and could hardly believe it. Piper MC was doing an interview on the Music Entertainment channel. He was dressed in all white, with more tattoos than I recalled. At the end of the chat, with his right hand he formed the letter C and with his left he flashed the number two, and then the number one. Few people will probably ever understand why Piper always does that. But I do.

"Look at Piper," I said to myself, feeling a grin on my face as I watched him talk.

I wanted to call Raq. "Can you believe it?" I longed to say.

But when I'd tried to call her after I got back home from New York, her phone went straight to voice mail, the box full.

A few days later, I had tried again. But I got a recording saying the phone was no longer in service.

As for school, Raq never came back. And I never resumed my place with the Fan Five. Raq may not have been the best friend I wanted her to be in the end, but my relationship with those girls had never felt right either. I was still looking for something real, for an honest connection with friends. And I was willing to hang by myself until I found that. My seatmate in anatomy, Corrine Carter, was back from being sick with bronchitis, so occasionally I chatted with her, but that was about it. Since I was on punishment for the rest of my natural life, it wasn't like I was desperate for people to hang with anyhow. It was just me, Gramma, and homework for the foreseeable future. And I was fine with that, to be honest.

"When I'm ready to let you out of the house again, you can get a job to pay back Judge and Kitty," Gramma had said. I tried to tell her I hadn't stolen the money, but she quickly pointed out that I had lived off of it for a week, and I couldn't argue with that. She was right. I'd made a mistake, but I also didn't want to spend the rest of my life feeling as miserable about it as I did. Hopefully returning the money would help.

¤ ✠ ¤

I always knew Piper was wonderful, from the first time I heard his voice, but *especially* after the first time I saw him perform live. I can still see him, his fist raised in the air . . .

"Yo . . . Y'all could've been anywhere in the world tonight . . ."

No, we couldn't have, Pipe. Most of us were stuck right there in Toledo, had nowhere else in the world to be. I was just lucky, I guess. I had a friend named Raq who wouldn't take no for an answer and you let us into your world because of her. Thank you.

And thank you, too, Gee. For everything.

I'm going to be watching the Grammy Awards every year waiting, hoping, I promise!

The Soul Train Music Award, too. Make that all of the awards shows.

Wonder if Buckstarr will be there with them. . . .

I used to ponder whether Piper ever even thought about me after that crazy week we spent together, if he would even know my name should our paths ever cross again. After all, no picture exists of the four of us, no actual proof of those days that we spent together. I don't know how we forgot to even take one, but I wish I had one snapshot to post on my bedroom door.

⬦✦⬦

It was a Tuesday evening in May, a week before then end of the school year , and I was in my room doing homework. I heard the announcement on the radio about a hot new single, a debut CD in stores today.

"Dirt." That was the name of the song.

Immediately, I knew it was Piper. And I loved it. Not just because the lyrics made so much sense, about how chasing money is the worst mind trip of them all, the most detrimental to relationships, to our culture, to our race—to the human race. That's all good.

No, I loved that song because of a line somewhere in the middle . . .

> *Don't get me wrong about dirt,*
> *nice things don't hurt,*
> *I've known things that shine.*
> *Yo . . . Glitz once was a friend of mine . . .*

Ha!

I'll never forget you, too, Piper!

And I'll never stop buying your music.

⬦✦⬦

On another day in May, soon after, me and Gramma pulled up at a red light on our way to church. I did a double-take.

Right next to us, a girl was sitting in her car, Latina and fabulous, looking in the rearview, fixing her hair, singing along to a song on the radio, loud enough for us to hear . . .

But it wasn't her.

Of course not.

Raq had gone away to the Juvenile Detention Center months ago, after our time on the road, after she was charged with theft in the second degree and possession of stolen property for the credit cards she lifted from her job and the money she stole from Judge and Kitty.

We were so busy chasing what was real, and then came reality. Juvie.

Still, I prefer to imagine that Raq is out there somewhere, that she's free.

She's so busy rehearsing for tours.

Yeah. That's why I haven't heard from her. That's it.

Maybe I'll never see her again.

Maybe it's best if I never do.

Raquel Marissa Diaz.

Mi hermana forever . . .

Whatever she's doing, I just hope she's okay.

And I hope she's still singing!

Then again, I know she is.

Acknowledgments

⬡ ◼ ⬡

To God be the glory. I am so thankful for His blessings, the opportunity to—again—use the talent that He has entrusted me with, and for the following people in my life:

Mom and Dad—Philip and Patricia Boles—you believed in me first and through it all and that has made all the difference. I am so blessed to be your daughter. My sister, Ginger, you always believe in me, support me, and have my back! Jada Marie, my niece, my friend, my honest critic, and the greatest junior consultant in the world. ☆ I love and appreciate you all so much!

Joy Peskin, you saw something in *Glitz*—and in me as an author—and it is my honor, my delight, and great fortune to work with such an enthusiastic, smart, witty, talented, and hip-as-all-get-out editor! *Yo, thank you for having faith in my talent and inspiring me so much.* ☆ I simply could not have done it without you, nor would I have ever wanted to. Ever.

Thank you to Regina Hayes, President and Publisher extraordinaire, for your enthusiasm and stamp of confidence in *Glitz*'s story as well as in me, as one of your authors. I am so grateful. Thank you also and sincerely to Leila Sales, Janet Pascal, Rachelle Mandik, and the entire Viking family. I am truly honored to have such a remarkable and legendary publishing home.

To Fonda Snyder, a writer's Godsend. You inspire me to keep writing, to keep growing, and to stay true to my creative heart. For so much—your hard work, diligence, and encouraging ways specifically—I sincerely thank you (for everything). Here's to a million more air toasts!

For your gracious support and/or other reasons that you know, my gratitude simply cannot be measured to: Michael and Joan Myers (<u>and families</u>), Sybil Wilkes, Arika Cason, Richard Messer, Fred Zackel, Anna Webman, Charlotte Sheedy, Meredith Kaffel, Pamela Nelson, Krystal Nelson, Maya Rock, Patty Gary Cox, Jackie Kallen, Amara Wagner, Angelique Pickett-Henderson, Paula Chase Hyman (and everyone from 28 Days Later), Chris Champion, Tracy Trivas, Cheryl Renee Herbsman, Cousino Crawford, Cydney Rax, Brodi Caldwell, Mia Strong, and my awesome Godson whom I love so much, Kameron "The Brave" Graves!

I am so honored and grateful to have studied the craft of writing with amazing instructors and equally amazing classmates and workshop peers at both Bowling Green State University and Stonybrook Southampton. Thank you to my wonderful SCBWI family and the incredible Authors Guild! Thank you, too, and *especially*, to Media Bistro—a dreamland for writers—and every person in our workshop with Joy that lovely Saturday afternoon.

To my supportive family, please insert your name here _____ so that my publisher doesn't faint from the ten page list of names I would otherwise have to submit. I love <u>each of you</u>, but most especially *you*, the one who just wrote your name! ☆ Thank you!!!

To all of my *Little Divas* across the country who waited so patiently for a sequel, and particularly those of you who are now old enough to read *Glitz*, I hope this will instead meet your cheerful page turns and that you will continue to believe in me. Thank you for all the letters. You have kept me inspired, and oh-my-goodness laughing, and I love you *all* so very much! I mean it.☆

And to Mel Berger, with all my heart and gratitude, always.